Into the
Wilderness

MYSTERY
and the
MINISTER'S
WIFE

Into the
Wilderness

TRACI DEPREE

GUIDEPOSTS
NEW YORK, NEW YORK

Into the Wilderness

ISBN-13: 978-0-8249-4799-6

Published by Guideposts
16 East 34th Street
New York, New York 10016
www.guideposts.com

Distributed by Ideals Publications, a division of Guideposts
2636 Elm Hill Pike, Suite 120
Nashville, Tennessee 37214

Library of Congress Cataloging-in-Publication Data

DePree, Traci

  Into the wilderness / Traci Depree.
      p. cm. — (Mystery and the minister's wife)
    ISBN 978-0-8249-4799-6
  1. Spouses of clergy—Fiction. 2. Clergy—Fiction. 3. Campers (Persons)
  —Fiction. 4. Wilderness areas—Fiction. 5. Great Smoky Mountains
  (N.C. and Tenn.)—Fiction. I. Title.
    PS3604.E67I58 2010
    813'.6—dc22

                                    2009024935

Cover by Lookout Design Group
Interior design by Cris Kossow
Typeset by Nancy Tardi

Printed and bound in the United States of America
10 9 8 7 6 5 4 3 2 1

For Caitlin

Chapter One

With the coming of autumn, nights were getting colder in the mountains surrounding Copper Mill, Tennessee. The trees had turned from vibrant green to shades of honey, amber, crimson, chestnut and rust. Kate Hanlon opened the window above the light table in her small stained-glass studio. The breeze floated gently into the room, stirring wisps of her strawberry blonde hair. She breathed deeply as she caught a refreshing tang of fallen leaves. Kate straightened on her stool, stretching to release the tension that had built up from hours of bending over her work. She had been working on a new piece, a pastoral scene of a horse in a pasture. It was a commissioned job for one of the nearby horse farms. She'd promised to have it ready for her client by the following weekend, but at this rate, that wasn't going to happen. She'd been putting in long hours to complete it, but there were so many intricate cuts and curved edges that it required more time than a simpler design.

She'd finished a series of smaller projects to sell at Smith Street Gifts the previous week. She'd sold so many windows and candleholders and lampshades at the shop that she'd needed to replenish that inventory as well.

She wiped her forehead, careful to use the back of her hand in case there were any glass shards on her palm. Glass cuts were a hazard of the job and the reason she stocked a hefty supply of Band-Aids.

The sound of her husband clearing his throat at the door drew her attention. Paul was still in exercise clothes from his morning run, and his salt-and-pepper hair was rumpled and stood at spiked angles.

"Sorry to disrupt your train of thought, but I was hoping you had an opinion . . . ," he said.

He held up two backpacks, one a vivid orange with soft sides and the other a dark forest green with an aluminum frame.

Kate glanced at her artwork, then back at Paul. "Can it wait?" she asked, not wanting to interrupt her work.

His face fell, and she felt a pang of guilt.

"Okay, okay," she said before taking a deep breath. "My opinion? Orange is definitely your color." She offered him a cheesy grin.

"That wasn't what I was looking for," he protested as his face broke into a smile. "I'm serious. Which one do you think I should take?"

Paul had been planning the first annual Faith Briar men's Smoky Mountains National Park camping and hiking outing for more than a month. He'd made campsite reservations, bought numerous maps and guides, and scoured Web sites for tips on the best sights to see. He'd prepared itineraries for the three-day event that seven men from Faith Briar Church had signed up to attend, and he had written morning devotionals to share at the start of each day.

Kate studied his handsome face. His vivid blue eyes met her warm brown ones as he waited for an answer. Finally she said, "You're only going on day hikes. It's not as if you're hauling your tent and sleeping bag with you everywhere you go. Why did you buy that big pack anyway?"

Paul lifted up the green backpack so he could admire it. "I thought you'd be proud of me. It was fifty percent off! Besides, I figure if we ever go on a longer trip, say to Glacier, I'll be all set."

"Glacier," Kate deadpanned. She loved teasing her husband. "I doubt I'll be backpacking in Montana anytime soon, honey!"

"I can be pretty persuasive," he winked at her. "Anyway, I think this trip will be a great male-bonding time with some of the guys from church."

"I think you've mentioned that a few times." She laughed.

"Come on." He motioned for her to follow. "I want to show you what I have laid out for tomorrow."

Kate glanced longingly toward her already-late project, then said, "All right. I'll humor you. At least I'll get some work done on this piece while you're gone. I have a deadline to meet!"

Paul clapped a hand to his heart. "Is that why you're so eager for me to go? Because I'm in your way? I'm offended!"

She slid off her stool and met him at the doorway, lifting on her toes to kiss his cheek. "Come on. Let's see what you have." Then she followed him into the master bedroom.

On the bed, he had laid out all the possible accoutrements of a camping and hiking adventure, including hygienic items, waterproof matches, a large Sam's Club-sized box of Nature Valley granola bars, his prescription allergy medication and weekly vitamin pillbox, extra Ziploc bags, several bandannas, a first-aid kit, a large Sharpie marker, a thermal first-aid blanket, sunscreen and bug repellant, a canteen, a collapsible cup that was still in its plastic wrap, a pile of assorted hiking clothes and shoes, a sleeping bag that would keep him warm well below freezing, the tent he'd purchased just for the trip, and his Coleman stove. Kate reached for an ivory-handled pocketknife that lay next to a tin plate and cup set.

"Are you sure you want to take this?" she asked, holding up the knife. "It means so much to you. I'd hate to see anything happen to it."

When Paul had achieved the rank of Eagle Scout as a senior in high school, the knife had been a treasured gift from his scoutmaster.

Paul shrugged. "It doesn't do me much good sitting in a drawer, does it? Besides, I've managed to hang on to it more than forty years now. I'd rather put it to good use. And it reminds me to be ever vigilant and 'leave no trace.'" He smiled. "Do you think I need to take these?" He held up a packet of iodine tablets.

"What are they for?"

"Purifying water."

"Honey," Kate said, "these are day hikes, remember? You're taking bottled water."

Paul shrugged and tossed the packet onto the dresser.

Kate scanned the items on the bed again. "You look ready to me. But there's no way you can fit all this gear into that small backpack."

"The pack is for while we're hiking. I have this"—he hoisted one of Kate's large, soft leather suitcases onto the bed—"for camp."

"Well, then, you obviously don't need me." Kate shrugged. "You're the Eagle Scout."

"True. Plus," Paul added, "who knows what dangerous creatures may be lurking in the wilderness—bears, mountain lions . . . Sam Gorman, Eli Weston." He let out a hearty laugh, and Kate smiled.

"Boys will always be boys," Kate said, then leaned in to kiss his cheek. "Looks like you've got everything under control here, camper. But let me know if you need anything else from me."

He raised his hand in a salute, and Kate smiled. Just as she turned to head back to her studio, the sound of a car in the driveway pulled her attention to the window.

"Who in the world?" She drew aside the curtains and spotted a red convertible with the top down. A pretty blonde wearing a Tennessee Bucs ball cap was looking around eagerly from the passenger seat.

A squeal of delight escaped Kate's lips. "I can't believe it!"

"What is it?" Paul said, but Kate was already on her way to the front door.

"It's Rebecca!" she called back. Kate had already swung the door open and was hurrying down the steps toward the car.

"What are you doing here?" she called to her youngest daughter.

Rebecca Hanlon's gaze met her mother's, and she broke into a huge grin. "Surprise!" she shouted, then jumped out of the car and flew to Kate for a hug. Paul was behind them, standing in the open doorway.

"You came all the way from New York without telling us?" he said, heading toward the vehicle.

"It's a surprise, Daddy!" She lifted on tiptoes to hug her father and kiss his cheek.

"Consider us surprised!" he exclaimed with a smile.

Kate had been so overcome with joy that she hadn't noticed the trim, good-looking man in the car with Rebecca. He opened the door and climbed out, a shy smile crossing his face.

"I hope you'll forgive us for not calling," he said.

"Oh, Mom, Daddy." Rebecca turned and placed a hand on the young man's shoulder. "This is Marcus Kingsley. He's an actor like me."

Kate noted the blush in her daughter's cheeks when she gazed at Marcus.

Kate smiled and held out a hand to him. "I'm happy to meet you."

Rebecca hadn't mentioned the young actor to her, and Kate wondered why. They talked on the phone weekly.

Marcus dipped his head in greeting and shook Kate's hand. "Becky has told me so much about you."

Kate had never heard anyone call her daughter by that name. It had always been Rebecca, even in grade school. She glanced at her daughter, who was grinning at Marcus with adoring eyes, and knew at that moment that he was no casual acquaintance. Rebecca obviously had feelings for him. Kate turned to Paul, who was also studying the young man. He held out a hand.

"I'm Rebecca's father. What was your name?"

"Marcus Kingsley."

His voice was rich and full, definitely an actor's voice, and his smile reached his hazel eyes. Kate imagined he was also a singer, given the melodious cadence of his speaking voice.

"Becky and I are . . . good friends," he said, then winked at Rebecca. She reached for his hand.

"Actually, we're dating," she said.

"Really?" Paul asked. He ran his fingers through his hair, then placed his hand on his hip.

"I wanted to tell you in person," Rebecca said. "Coming spur of the moment like this was Marcus' idea. He really wanted to meet you, so we took off work and here we are!" She gave them a sheepish grin.

"How long have you two been dating?" Paul asked.

Kate knew his tone; he'd used it often enough when the girls had brought home new boyfriends in the past. It was the interrogation tone, slightly intimidating with overtones of "I'll decide whether I approve of you when the questioning is finished."

"Oh," Rebecca said, a big grin still pasted on her face as if she hadn't noticed her father's tone. "We've been going out a couple of months. Marcus helped me get the waitressing job at the Empire State Café. He's a cook there."

Paul cleared his throat and looked at Marcus. "So you're an actor?"

"Yes, sir," Marcus said.

Paul's gaze moved to Rebecca, and his face relaxed slightly. "So . . . how long are you planning to stay? The week?"

His gaze traveled to Kate, and she knew immediately that he'd remembered his camping plans. They hadn't seen Rebecca in ages; for him to leave the next day would be impossible.

"Well, a long weekend, really. We have to be back to work by Thursday morning," Rebecca said. "So we'll head for home early Wednesday." She squeezed Marcus' hand and gazed at him lovingly.

Kate had to admit that she'd rarely seen a man as good looking. With that five o'clock shadow, dark hair, and perfectly straight teeth, he reminded her of Hugh Jackman, an actor she'd seen in a Broadway show the last time she and Paul had visited New York City. Marcus' dark looks were a striking complement to Rebecca's fair-skinned beauty, her long blonde hair, and her father's vivid blue eyes. She was as pretty as any high-fashion model, and as tall. She had surpassed her mother's five feet, six inches in seventh grade and now nearly matched her father's height of five feet, eleven.

"When did you leave New York?" Paul asked.

"Last night," Rebecca said.

"You drove all night? You must be tired," Kate said, leading the way into the house. "I'll put on a pot of coffee. Do you drink coffee, Marcus?"

"Yes, ma'am," Marcus said, that irresistible smile in place.

"Our showing up unannounced isn't a problem, is it?" Rebecca asked as she turned to look at her father. No doubt she had seen his strained expression.

They moved into the tiny kitchen and gathered around the L-shaped counter. Pots and pans hung from the ceiling in true Food Network fashion, despite the seventies-era feel of the rest of the room. Across from the counter was an old oak dining-room table that had been the centerpiece of many family meals over the years.

Kate and Paul exchanged an awkward glance as Rebecca and Marcus sat down at the table, then Kate squeezed past Paul to the coffeemaker.

"Uh oh," Rebecca said. "Did you have plans for the next few days?" She looked at her father who was taking a chair next to her at the table. When he didn't say anything, she shifted her gaze to Kate.

"Well," Kate began as she filled the coffeemaker with cold water, then pulled down a can of Folgers from the cupboard and lifted the lid. The scent of ground, roasted coffee wafted into the air. "Your father was scheduled to lead a men's group from church to the Smokies for a few days of hiking. He's been planning it forever—"

"It's okay," Paul interrupted. "How often do I get to see my favorite girl?"

"Oh, Daddy, I'm so sorry!" Rebecca said. "I should have called first. It was just that when Marcus suggested coming to meet you, I got so excited about surprising you that I didn't think about your plans."

"I feel awful," Marcus added, shaking his head.

Paul patted Rebecca's hand. "Really, it's okay. Sam Gorman can take the group. I'll just give him my notes—"

"That's my daddy, making notes for a simple weekend camping trip!" Rebecca laughed and turned to Marcus, whose gaze had shifted toward the window.

Kate thought he seemed preoccupied with something, and wondered what it could be. She poured the coffee into the machine, closed the lid, and hit the Start button.

"My dad was such a Boy Scout when I was growing up," Rebecca went on as Marcus returned his gaze to her. "He used to type up these long notes before every vacation so we'd know the historical background of wherever we were going. Like when we went to Gettysburg, he gave us a fifteen-page report on the place and then quizzed us before we could leave the driveway!"

Marcus laughed good-naturedly, then glanced out the window again. Kate followed his gaze and decided that he must be enjoying the fall view.

"It was educational," Paul protested, chuckling.

"No kidding!" Rebecca said, nudging her father.

"So," Kate said, turning to Marcus, "how did you two meet?"

Marcus reached for Rebecca's hand, the dimples in his cheeks like parentheses. "Becky and I were both auditioning for parts in a small off-Broadway show. She, of course, was spectacular! Well . . . long story short, neither of us got the parts, but we got to talking—"

"Marcus has the most amazing singing voice!" Rebecca interrupted. "Sing something for them, honey."

Marcus blushed.

Kate tried to suppress a flinch when her daughter called him "honey." She'd never heard Rebecca use pet names with any of her previous boyfriends, and Marcus was practically a total stranger. Then she had to remind herself that he wasn't a stranger to Rebecca.

"You're embarrassing him, Rebecca!" Kate admonished.

"He's an actor, Mom. He likes the attention."

Marcus gave Rebecca a slight shake of his head. "Another time, hon."

"Okay, fine. Another time," Rebecca said with a pout.

"Rebecca's the one who likes attention," Paul said to Marcus. "Have you noticed that already? Give her the slightest bit of interest, and she's on it like a hound on a fox—"

"Anyway," Rebecca cut in, ignoring her father's jab, "we went out for coffee afterward, and Marcus told me about the job opening at the Empire State Café."

Rebecca had phoned Kate in July with the news that she'd gotten the full-time waitressing job, but she hadn't mentioned a new love interest. Kate glanced at the young couple. Rebecca sat a little too close to her man, holding his hand and sending those tender glances Kate had seen when her two older children had been dating their future spouses.

It troubled her, though, that Rebecca had never mentioned him in their weekly conversations. Why had she held this news back?

"Is that café *in* the Empire State Building?" Paul asked Marcus.

"No, it's a little hole in the wall on Fifth Avenue," Marcus said. "Nothing impressive, but working there pays the bills, you know?"

"So you're a cook?" Kate asked.

Marcus nodded. "A skill I picked up along the way."

"You'll find that Marcus has many hidden talents," Rebecca said.

Chapter Two

Marcus went outside to retrieve their bags from the car, and Paul returned to the bedroom to put away his camping gear. Kate and Rebecca wandered out to the backyard, just off the living room, and stood under a beautiful old maple tree. Its crimson leaves glimmered in the sunlight and complemented the golds and ambers in the woods behind the house.

The backyard reflected the beauty of their country surroundings, with its many potted plants and Kate's little touches here and there. Some of the flowers had lost their blooms, except the mums that were abundant at this time of year. Kate had a variety of colors: orange, white and purple.

She and Rebecca sat down at a black wrought-iron table on a small patio area just outside the sliding-glass door.

She glanced at her daughter, who lifted her face to the warming day.

Leaves fluttered down from the branches of the maple tree at intervals, carried by a gentle breeze, and a squirrel chattered at them from a high tree branch. They'd brought along leftover bread crusts that Kate kept for feeding the animals. Rebecca tossed a piece toward the tree, and the squirrel edged its way down to retrieve it.

"This is nice," Rebecca said, smiling at her mother.

Kate tugged her sweater around her shoulders, more from habit than from feeling chilled.

They enjoyed the quiet for a moment before Rebecca said, "It's so good to see you, Mom. I've missed you."

Kate reached over to squeeze her daughter's hand, and the comfortable silence descended again. It was a lovely day. The breeze whispered through the leaves overhead, and occasionally one would waft down in a lazy arc to the ground.

"Hey," Rebecca finally said, "do you have the ring Gran left me? Or is it in a safe-deposit box?"

Kate's grandmother had bequeathed a very valuable sapphire-and-diamond ring to Rebecca when she died. As the youngest of Kate's children, Rebecca had been a favorite of the eccentric woman, who liked to shower her with gifts, though none as expensive and exquisite as the ring. The appraiser had valued it at almost ten thousand dollars. When Rebecca had decided to go to New York, Kate and Paul had agreed to keep it in safekeeping until she felt settled and safe enough to store it herself.

"It's here," Kate said, "in my bedroom. Why?"

Rebecca shrugged. "Oh, I told Marcus about it, and he said he'd love to see it."

Kate glanced up at her daughter. Something didn't seem quite right about that. She raised an eyebrow but didn't voice her thoughts. Instead, she cleared her throat and said, "So, honey, I can tell you really like Marcus. Why didn't you tell me about him before now?"

Rebecca tossed another piece of crust onto the ground and watched as the squirrel enjoyed the free meal.

"I guess we've just been getting to know each other . . . It's all happened so fast, really." She lifted her face to the warm sun. "He's . . ."—she took a deep breath—"I don't know. He's smart and funny and talented and . . ." She shrugged. "You know? I really, *really* like him."

"You haven't known him that long."

"I know it's only been two months, but I feel like I've known him a lot longer."

"Has he always been a New Yorker?"

Rebecca shook her head. "He was raised in New Jersey. He has three older siblings—two brothers and a sister. His folks split up when he was young."

"I'm sorry," Kate said.

"He doesn't talk about it much. I mean, I haven't even met them yet. And they live in New Jersey."

"Really? Even though they live that close?"

"We've just been so busy with work and auditions that we haven't had time to go. But I'm going to make sure we pay them a visit right after we get home. It's just ridiculous that we haven't done it yet." She sighed and glanced at the squirrel that was chattering at them from the base of the tree.

"Marcus really believes in me, you know? He believes

in my talent," Rebecca went on. She lifted her gaze to her mother, and Kate recognized the unasked questions that lingered in the air. *Why don't you believe in me, Mom? Why don't you want me to succeed?*

Kate knew that her daughter craved her approval of her acting career. But there were so many hazards that came with fame and wealth—potential for drugs and alcoholism, pride and greed, not to mention the challenges the career placed on one's faith. In light of all that, Kate was nervous about Rebecca's pursuing it.

Yet she also knew that her daughter was phenomenally talented. Rebecca poured her heart into every performance, and the girl could sing better than anyone Kate had ever heard, big-time performers included. She had no doubt that her daughter could do well in acting if given the right opportunity. Still, she prayed that God would guard Rebecca's heart.

"So, how is Marcus' spiritual life?" Kate asked point-blank.

"Come on, Mom. We're just dating!" Rebecca said.

"His faith is important," Kate insisted. "You know how much faith matters in marriage. Marriage isn't always easy, and different faith perspectives make it that much more challenging. I just don't want to see you get hurt."

Rebecca had given her heart to Christ during summer camp at the tender age of eleven. Kate thought about that homecoming. Rebecca had been so thrilled about her newfound faith that she told anyone and everyone who would listen that they needed to know Jesus too.

"He's a Christian, Mom," Rebecca said.

"How do you know?" Kate leaned in and studied her daughter's face. Rebecca's eyes darted back and forth as she searched for the right words. It raised alarm bells in Kate's head. Was Rebecca being completely honest with herself about this young man and his relationship with God? Or was she allowing his good looks and suave manner to sway her?

"We've talked about it," she finally said. "He even comes to church with me sometimes."

"Sometimes?" Kate probed.

"He's a cook at a café, Mom. Sometimes he has to work Sundays. You know, you have to trust me and let me grow up."

"I'm not saying I don't trust you," Kate said, keeping her tone calm to prevent the conflict from escalating. Her daughter had many wonderful qualities, but even-temperedness was not one of them. But she knew this was an important time to express her feelings to Rebecca. In some ways, she thought, raising her children never ended.

"Yes, Mom, you are saying you don't trust me. Otherwise you wouldn't have asked."

"I asked Melissa and Andrew the same question when they were dating their future spouses, so it's only fair I ask you too. Besides, we knew their significant others pretty well by that time." She paused, then had a flash of intuition. "Has Marcus proposed?"

Rebecca shrugged, though the blush that spread

across her cheeks said enough. "We've talked about it," she finally admitted.

Kate couldn't believe her ears. Her baby girl had talked about marriage with a man Kate didn't even know. She tried to comprehend it and felt hurt that Rebecca hadn't confided in her.

"Did you tell anyone, honey, or were you just going to elope?" Kate paused, then asked, "Are you living together?"

"No, Mom! I've told Melissa that we've talked about getting married, but—"

"Oh, Rebecca." Kate sighed. "We don't even know this young man."

"But *I* do, Mom! And I love him!"

Her blue eyes met Kate's, and Kate could see the wounded expression in them. Yet she knew Rebecca could be an emotional roller coaster of highs and lows. She had the capacity to love deeply . . . and to be hurt deeply. Kate placed a calming hand on Rebecca's arm.

"I'm not trying to make you feel bad. I just want to protect you, to help you make a good choice. This is one of the most important decisions you'll ever make in life. I'm not saying that I don't like Marcus. I just don't *know* him."

"So get to know him!" Rebecca shot back. "That's why we came this weekend, Mom."

She reached out to clasp her daughter's hand. "And your dad and I are so happy you came, Rebecca." She smiled, her thoughts suddenly turning to Paul, who was in the bedroom, putting away his camping gear so he could spend time with his little girl, like the devoted father he was.

"What is it?" Rebecca prompted.

"Oh, it's nothing," Kate said.

"No," Rebecca said, "I know that look. Something's on your mind."

"Well," Kate glanced toward the house to see if anyone was coming. "You should've seen your dad getting ready for his trip. He was really excited. He'd even pulled out his old Eagle Scout knife."

"Oh, I feel awful! We should've called, Mom. It's just that Marcus seemed so eager to meet you. I'd never seen him like that before. He wanted to get in the car and go right away. I mean, we'd talked about driving down some-day so he could meet you, but . . ." She shrugged. "And now we've ruined Dad's plans. He should still go. Marcus and I can visit with you. You can get to know Marcus while Dad's camping."

"You know your father would never agree to that."

They paused in thought. The squirrel had finally finished devouring the two crusts of bread and had scam-pered back up the tree.

Finally Rebecca broke the silence. "I have an idea. Maybe Marcus could go with Dad on his trip. Then they can get to know each other one-on-one. Dad will see what a great guy Marcus is, and you and I can have some mother-daughter time."

Kate had to admit she liked the idea, especially since it would give Paul a chance to get acquainted with Marcus without Rebecca running interference. He could really get to know the young man, find out if his intentions were honorable.

"I'll see what your dad thinks," Kate said. "Are you sure Marcus would be up for it?"

"He'll do anything I ask him to," she said, a pleased smile crossing her face.

WHILE REBECCA WENT TO TALK to Marcus about the idea, Kate went to find Paul. Like a defeated warrior, he stood over the camping paraphernalia that still covered the bed. Kate touched his hand, and he glanced up at her.

"Disappointed?" she asked.

He nodded. "But I'm glad to see my girl."

"Did you know that Marcus and Rebecca have talked about marriage?"

Paul lifted an eyebrow. "What? We don't even know this guy! Did you notice how he kept looking out the window and didn't make eye contact?"

"He's in unfamiliar surroundings and on approval," Kate pointed out. "I think we're just sensitive that our daughter has fallen in love with a man who is a total stranger to us. She says he's a great guy, that he's kind to her and goes to church with her . . ."

"How many times has Rebecca said that about a guy she's dating?" Paul said with a laugh. "She loves every one right up until she breaks up with him."

"But she's never mentioned marriage before," Kate reminded him.

Paul nodded, then crossed his arms over his chest as his gaze returned to his camping supplies. A frown furrowed his brow. "I hate disappointing the guys at the church."

Kate slipped an arm around his waist. "Rebecca had an idea, and I think it's a good one."

Paul waited for her to go on.

"How about if you take Marcus on the camping trip? It'll give you a chance to get to know him one-on-one while Rebecca and I spend some mother-daughter time together."

Paul rubbed his chin and raised his eyebrows as he considered the proposal.

"Rebecca said he'd do anything she asks, and it does seem like he really wanted to meet us. It makes me wonder if his excitement has anything to do with a marriage proposal. She even asked about Gran's ring," Kate added.

Finally he spoke. "I guess it wouldn't hurt, would it?" His smile returned. "But I wanted to spend time with Rebecca too."

"I know, but with a boyfriend here, how much quality time would you get with her anyway? Besides, this will be good for Rebecca and me."

Paul grinned. "You're just kicking me out of the house, aren't you?"

"Of course I am." Kate gave him a devious wink. "Hey, I'm not getting to work on my stained glass either, so the least you can do is entertain your future son-in-law." Kate felt the weight of her deadline tugging on her conscience, but she was determined to put it out of her mind for the next few days and enjoy the time with Rebecca.

"We'll see about that. He's still on approval!" Paul laughed. "You need the break, anyway, Katie." He kissed her forehead. "You've been working too hard."

"I agree. Time with Rebecca is just the reprieve I needed."

"And we'll just see if this guy is really good enough for my daughter!"

AFTER A LUNCH of egg-salad sandwiches, Kate and Rebecca spent the day helping the men gather all the supplies Marcus would need for the trip. Paul had many of the items in duplicate, so there wasn't much they needed to purchase in Pine Ridge. And since Marcus had packed for the long weekend anyway, he had a fair assortment of clothing, though they had to stop by a shoe store to buy hiking boots. By late afternoon, he was packed and ready for the next morning's adventure.

Rebecca and the two men retired to the living room and reclined on the sofa while Kate went to the kitchen to fix them something to drink. A few minutes later, she reappeared with four glasses of iced tea on a serving tray. As she set down the tray, she noticed Marcus whispering something to Rebecca. Paul was skimming the latest *Scouting* magazine, but Kate could tell by the way he kept glancing at them that he was actually observing their interactions.

Rebecca smiled up at her mother when Kate handed her a glass of tea. "Do you mind getting that ring now, Mom?" Rebecca asked, then glanced at Marcus.

"Oh," Kate said. "Sure, honey."

She padded to the master bedroom and returned carrying a red-velvet box.

When Rebecca opened the lid, Marcus leaned in to look.

"Wow! It's beautiful," he said. "Just like you told me."

Kate noticed Marcus' intense stare, and she wondered if perhaps he had considered buying Rebecca a ring or if he would ask to give her this one.

Rebecca lifted the ring out of its box and slipped it onto her finger. "I don't know what Gran was thinking when she left it to me."

"She was thinking that she loved you," Kate said as she settled into an overstuffed chair that flanked the couch and reached for her glass of tea. The sweet tea tasted perfect after a day of shopping, packing, and chatting.

Marcus seemed like a nice enough fellow. He was cordial and polite. He made conversation easily and was quick to ask questions. Kate watched as he and Rebecca admired the ring's sapphire and diamond.

"We should really take that to the bank," Paul said, "and put it in our safe-deposit box with our passports and birth certificates."

"I know," Kate admitted. "I had sort of forgotten about its value. I tend to think we're pretty secure here in Copper Mill, though I'm not sure what would make me think *that*." She laughed, and Paul joined her.

The amount of trouble Kate had gotten into because of her frequent sleuthing had become an inside joke. Thankfully, they could laugh instead of cry, because they had always managed to escape any real injury.

"Do you know how much it's worth?" Marcus asked,

after waiting for Kate and Paul's laughter to wane. The question struck Kate as inappropriate.

"We've had it appraised, yes," she said, avoiding a direct answer to the question. "Say," she said, changing the subject, "we were wondering if we could treat the two of you to a nice supper before the men head into the wilderness tomorrow. There's a great restaurant called the Bristol."

"We always enjoy a nice meal," Rebecca said as she turned to look first at Marcus, then at her father. "Especially if it's free!"

Kate noticed that Marcus looked strangely nervous.

"Let's take the convertible!" Rebecca suggested. "I love that car, but it's a good thing I have Marcus, because I have no idea how to drive a stick."

"If it's okay with you, Marcus, I'll drive," Paul volunteered. "It's been a long time since I've cruised in one of those babies."

Chapter Three

The Bristol was actually part of the newly restored Hamilton Springs Hotel, a resort and spa just down the road from Faith Briar Church. In its former life, it had been the historic Copper Creek Hotel, a rundown building that had lost its charm long ago, but now it was a grand two-story hotel.

The group climbed out of the convertible and made their way across the parking lot.

"I definitely want to get wheels like this if I ever buy myself a car," Rebecca said. "It was so much fun driving that thing here from New York, wasn't it Marcus?"

Marcus nodded and shot a smile her way. Kate pulled a comb from her oversized handbag to straighten her wind-blown hair. No wonder Rebecca had worn a ponytail.

Paul reached the entrance first and held the door open for everyone. The wide double doors opened onto a massive foyer with double staircases that wound up to the floor above. The foyer was painted in a warm honey tone, with a blazing fireplace at the center and mounted deer and elk trophies hanging from the polished wood walls. Thick, heavy beams lined the ceiling, and throughout the open space, intimate groupings of overstuffed furniture were arranged on woven Indian rugs, giving the room definition.

To the left of the foyer was the Bristol. Kate led the way into the restaurant, a light and airy room with banks of divided windows on three sides. The waitstaff bustled between tables, and the host, who was wearing a tailored suit, showed them to a table overlooking a pond.

"Is that table available?" Marcus asked, pointing to a table at the very back of the room. "It'll be more private," he added.

Kate exchanged a curious look with Paul, but neither said anything. They followed the maître d' to the table and took their seats. A server immediately deposited four glasses of water in front of them.

Rebecca turned to her father. "So, Dad, where exactly are you and Marcus going to be while you're on your trip?"

Kate glanced at Marcus. His attention was anywhere but on the conversation. His eyes scanned the room, then his gaze shifted outside to the back lawn and the pond. Rebecca placed a hand on his, and he turned his attention back to her. His shoulders relaxed, and he smiled vaguely.

"Sorry," he said. "It's so . . . pretty out there."

"You okay?" Kate heard Rebecca whisper to him in a low voice. "You've seemed so stressed today."

Marcus nodded and whispered, "I'm just fine."

"We have several destinations in mind," Paul said. "We'll start out of Gatlinburg and camp at the Elkmont

Campground, then hit the hot spots just south of there. Of course, we'll check out Newfound Gap, where the park was first dedicated by FDR, and Clingmans Dome, the highest point in the park. We might hike parts of the Appalachian Trail and the Alum Cave Trail. There's so much to see that we really can't do it all in three days, not if we want to get off the beaten path, anyway. I can't wait to get out and really experience the place."

Kate smiled at his contagious enthusiasm.

"It sounds awesome, doesn't it, Marcus?" Rebecca said, nudging him.

"It sounds like a lot of fun, Mr. Hanlon," Marcus agreed.

His eyes scanned the room one more time, then Kate saw them widen as if he was alarmed. She glanced to where he was looking and saw two men in dark suits talking to the seating host at the entrance. Their backs were facing Kate, so she couldn't see their faces, but they had shiny black hair that looked like it was slicked back with gel. By the time she looked back at Marcus, he had scooted his chair away from the table.

"What's going on?" Rebecca asked.

"I . . . uh," Marcus began. "If you'll excuse me, I need to use the restroom." Then he disappeared down the hall.

Kate exchanged looks with Paul and Rebecca. They had seen the men too.

"What was that all about?" Paul asked.

"He hasn't been himself lately," Rebecca admitted. "I think he's just stressed about an audition or something."

The two men at the front looked around the room, then left the restaurant without being seated. It seemed more than odd to Kate. Why had Marcus been so anxious to leave when he saw them?

LATER THAT NIGHT, Kate and Paul spoke in hushed tones as they turned down their sheets and got ready for bed. Rebecca was staying in the guest room that doubled as Paul's study, and Marcus was sleeping on the living room sleeper sofa.

"What do you think was wrong with Marcus tonight?" Kate asked as she ran a hand across the white sheets and untucked them. She fluffed the pillows, then went into the adjoining bathroom to put on her night cream.

"And did you see those men at the entrance?" Kate went on, not waiting for Paul to answer her first question. She raised her voice a notch so he could hear her from the bathroom. She looked at herself in the mirror and began slathering cream on her face.

"Yes, I did. Hard to know what to make of it," he said as he climbed into bed. "Marcus seemed fine after he came back."

"How can you say that? He was as nervous as a caged animal." Kate finished applying the cream, then twisted the cap onto the jar and returned to the bedroom. "Something's not right," she went on, standing alongside the bed. "He seems way too interested in Rebecca's ring too. Did you notice that? Why would he ask how much it was worth?"

"You're just imagining things." Paul raised an eyebrow. "She told him about the ring, and he said it looked pretty. That isn't all that odd, especially considering they're talking marriage."

"Yes, I thought of that. But you have to admit, the way he left the table . . ."

"Sure, it was abrupt, but let's give the guy the benefit of the doubt, okay? He must be exhausted after all that driving, not to mention he's here to win our approval because he cares for our daughter." Paul shrugged. "He seemed fairly comfortable here at the house. Maybe he has a fear of public places or something."

"He's an actor, Paul. He's in public places all the time."

"Maybe he's a good actor, then."

"Or a really bad one," Kate said. "Remember, Marcus said they didn't get those parts in that off-Broadway show they tried out for." She climbed into bed and tucked her pillow under her neck. The sheets felt cold against her legs.

"He and Rebecca seem to really enjoy each other," Paul offered.

"So, he's already won you over?" she teased.

"I didn't say that." Paul turned onto his side and looked at Kate. "We only just met him this morning. Rebecca cares for him, so that should count for something." He gave her a peck on the cheek, then rolled over, reached for the nightstand lamp, and plunged the room into darkness. "Besides," he said, "don't you remember how nervous I was when I first met your parents?"

Kate laughed at the memory. "You were shaking so hard! And my dad gave you the third degree. Can you believe he actually asked you how you expected to support me on a minister's salary?"

"I'd known him, what, thirty minutes by that time? I half expected him to pull out a lie detector or give me the drip torture!"

"I think he was considering it!" Kate chuckled.

"And look how things turned out." He turned and smiled at Kate, a look of tenderness in his eyes. "I don't know much about Marcus, but I do know that Rebecca likes him. So let's just give it some time."

Chapter Four

The next morning, as the crowd at church began to thin, the campers were busy getting ready to leave. Kate, Rebecca and Marcus watched as the hive of activity buzzed around them. Paul was coordinating everything from the center of the church parking lot, clipboard in hand as he checked off the list of supplies and campers. The gear he and Marcus brought lay on the ground alongside a rusted aqua fifteen-passenger van that one of the newer members of the church had lent them for the occasion.

Kate waved at Eli Weston as he walked to his truck. The thirty-four-year-old's shock of blond hair looked almost white in the brilliant morning sunshine. Kate assumed he had closed his antiques shop so he could go on the trip. He jumped in the cab of his truck, grabbed a green army duffel bag and a knapsack, and tossed them next to Paul and Marcus' gear.

"Did everyone remember to bring food?" Paul called out as he went through his list. He'd assigned each person a few grocery items and assorted kitchenware to bring on the trip so that when they got to the park, they would have all the supplies they'd need for meal preparation. Heads nodded around the group.

Sam Gorman, the church organist and Paul's good friend, deposited his gear on the ground next to the van. Sam also owned the local mercantile, and Kate knew that he'd arranged for his part-time staff to cover for him while he was gone. He opened the van's double doors and began loading baggage into the back. Marcus went over to help him and began handing Sam the duffels and backpacks from the growing pile.

Marcus had seemed more at ease that morning, though Kate hadn't missed how he'd glanced around the church when they'd first arrived. It was as if he was looking for someone. She wondered if perhaps he saw the men from the restaurant, but there had been no unfamiliar faces in church, aside from Marcus.

While Kate was lost in thought, Eli Weston approached and held out his hand to Rebecca.

"Rebecca, it's so nice to see you again," he said, a shy smile on his handsome face.

Rebecca shook hands with him and grinned, "It's good to see you again too."

Kate noticed the brief spark that passed between the two. Her eyes caught Eli's, and he blushed.

"Do you still live in New York?" he asked Rebecca.

"Of course, I'm still looking for that perfect role on Broadway. All part of being an actress."

"And a beautiful one," he said, though as soon as the words left his mouth, his face flamed bright red again.

Rebecca glowed at the praise.

"I . . . uh . . . I've always wanted to visit New York City," Eli said.

"Really?" Rebecca glanced at her mother, the grin returning to her face. "You should come out sometime. I'll show you the sights."

"That'd be amazing," Eli said.

Kate smiled at the two, then glanced over at Marcus, who was talking to Sam Gorman. The Jenner men— father Danny, seventeen-year-old James, and fourteen-year-old Justin—were hoisting their gear into the back of the van. Kate could see they were in a heated discussion. Danny's face was red, and James flung his gear with an almost violent force.

The men finished loading their gear and closed the doors of the van. Marcus stared at Eli with narrowed eyes, then made his way over to the group.

"It looks like we're about ready to hit the road," Marcus said, slipping an arm around Rebecca's waist. "I'm Marcus Kingsley." He shook hands with Eli, who introduced himself.

"Marcus is an actor too," Rebecca said.

Kate wondered why she hadn't introduced him as her

boyfriend, and by the puzzled look on Marcus' face, he was apparently wondering the same thing.

"I think we're good to go, Paul," Sam Gorman's voice drew their attention. "Did you remember the maps?"

Paul quickly felt his pockets as if he'd forgotten them. Then with a raised eyebrow and a twinkle in his eyes, he reached into the side pocket of his cargo shorts and pulled out the Tennessee state map as well as a map of Great Smoky Mountains National Park day hikes.

He'd almost worn the shorts to church that morning, but Kate had convinced him to change after the service instead. She hadn't seen him this excited about a trip since he'd gone to Wisconsin to see the Tommy Bartlett Water Ski Show when the kids were young.

"You know me better than that, Sam Gorman!" Paul said.

Sam turned away with a chuckle and winked at Kate. Just then Livvy Jenner, Copper Mill's town librarian and Kate's best friend, came up and gave Kate a hug.

"Hey, you," she said. "You think we'll miss these menfolk?"

Kate noticed the strained look on her face and wondered what was wrong.

"Are you kidding?" Kate said, patting her arm. "I thought we ladies could have tea tomorrow afternoon in celebration of a little peace and quiet."

Kate touched her daughter's sleeve, and Rebecca turned from talking with Marcus and Eli toward the women. "Rebecca, you remember my friend Livvy, don't you?"

Rebecca smiled sweetly at Kate's auburn-haired friend. "Hey, Livvy," she said. "How are you?"

"Oh, I'm doing well. What are you two up to this afternoon?" she asked.

"We're going to have lunch at the Country Diner and relax at home, I think," Kate said, then raised an eyebrow as she glanced at Rebecca, who nodded her approval. "Would you like to join us, Livvy?"

Kate thought it might give her a chance to talk to Livvy and fill her in.

"Thanks,"—Livvy cleared her throat—"but I have a book waiting at home with my name on it. It's a rare opportunity when I have the house to myself." Her gaze wandered to her husband and sons across the parking lot.

Kate pulled her aside and asked, "What's wrong?"

"James is being such a teenager!" Livvy said. "His father has gone to all this trouble to make this trip happen. Danny got preapproved absences for the boys from school so they could get their homework done ahead of time, and now James tells us that his garage band is having a concert, and he can't go on the trip."

"He doesn't want to go camping?"

Livvy shook her head. "Oh, he's going all right! I'm so tired of him making selfish choices. He has to think about someone else for a change. Lately he's been 'the band this and the band that.' I'm tired of it running our lives. Last night he got in late, and he hadn't even packed for the trip yet."

Kate squeezed Livvy's arm, and the gesture brought fresh tears to Livvy's eyes.

"Are you sure you don't want to join us for lunch?" Kate asked.

Livvy shook her head. "I'll be okay. Really." She blew out a long breath.

"Was Danny pretty upset?"

"Well, sure he was. You should've heard them going at it this morning. It was a lovely scene on our way to church!" She sighed and gazed down at the ground. "Danny and I have talked about making James drop out of the band, but who knows what that would do to him, or to our relationship with him. But he's gone so much, practicing and then to gigs. The band doesn't always play at places I'm comfortable with. Sometimes I just wonder about the negative influence this band might have on him."

Kate chuckled, and Livvy looked confused.

"Forgive me," Kate said. "You sound so much like me with Rebecca, it's not even funny."

Livvy smiled, and some of the tension in her face eased.

"So, how do you manage it?" Livvy asked.

"I pray a lot." She shrugged. "Sometimes I feel like there's not much else I can do."

"My thoughts exactly!" Livvy held her tall seventeen-year-old son in her gaze. He had moved to the side of the parking lot, arms still crossed in defiance, a sullen look on his face. "He's shown in so many ways that he can't manage the responsibility. His grades aren't what they should be, and I know it's because of all the time he's spending with the band."

"He is only seventeen," Kate reminded her friend. "Maybe it's too soon to let him have that much freedom. It's a judgment call, that's for sure."

"Yeah. I just hate for it to put a damper on Danny's time with the boys."

"How's Justin taking all of this?"

"He's oblivious." Livvy smiled. "He's been looking forward to this trip right along with his dad."

"James will come around," Kate assured her.

Livvy nodded, then Paul's voice drew their attention.

"All right. Is everyone here?" Paul beamed as he looked at his clipboard again. "I'm going to take roll. Say 'Howdy' when your name is called. Carl Wilson . . ."

Carl answered as directed, then the rest followed suit—Jack Wilson, Danny Jenner, Justin, James, Sam Gorman, Eli Weston, and Marcus Kingsley. Heads turned toward the newcomer when Paul said his name.

Paul cleared his throat and said, "Marcus is our daughter Rebecca's friend. He's visiting us for a few days, so I invited him to join us on our little adventure. I hope you'll make him feel welcome."

The men waved and offered words of greeting. Marcus smiled wide and waved in return. "Thanks," he said.

"Our goal today is to get to the park," Paul went on. "We'll eat lunch on the way, then stop at the Sugarlands Visitor Center outside of Gatlinburg, set up our camp at

Elkmont Campground, and make a light supper. We might do a short hike tonight. We'll be close to the Jakes Creek Trail, the Cucumber Gap Trail, and the Little River Trail. We'll see what we have time for. Sam will lead us in a brief worship time around the campfire each night, and James has agreed to play guitar for us." He glanced at James, who remained motionless.

Paul led the group in a prayer, asking for God's protection and blessing. Then it was time to go. The men said their farewells to their loved ones and climbed into the van. Paul was so busy getting everyone else set up that he forgot to say anything to Kate until she pulled him aside.

"Hey there. I think you're forgetting something after all," Kate teased.

"Sorry," he said with a sheepish grin. "You know how I am. I just get—"

"Focused?" she finished his sentence, a wry smile on her lips.

Paul nodded.

"Don't forget to take your allergy medication, okay?" Kate knew he usually relied on her to give him the meds whenever he needed them, so she could see him completely forgetting that he had them in his pack.

"I don't like them; they make me sleepy." Paul started with the same complaints he'd had when the pills had first been prescribed.

"But they make you less miserable."

"Okay, if I start attracting wild animals with my sneezing, I'll remember to take the pills." He smiled and bent to kiss her cheek, but Kate turned her head just in time to give him a smooch on the lips.

"Be careful, honey," she said. "You aren't as young as you used to be. Don't twist an ankle or anything. And remember, I love you . . . very much."

"I love you too, hon, and I'll be fine," he assured her. Then he turned to Rebecca and said, "I'll keep an eye on that boyfriend of yours, sweetheart."

She glanced at Marcus, offering him a shy smile, then she raised up on her toes and gave her father a peck on the cheek.

"Thanks, Daddy."

Kate stood back as Marcus and Rebecca said their good-byes. They held each other close, standing forehead to forehead.

"You take care of yourself," Rebecca said.

"Don't worry about me, honey. You just have a good visit with your mom." He smiled, and his dimples deepened. Then he gave her a kiss.

Kate looked at the ground, feeling as though she was intruding on their moment.

"Don't forget that I love you," Marcus said when she stepped out of his embrace.

"I love you too," Rebecca whispered. "Maybe someday this ring—" She looked down at her hand, then said in a panic-stricken voice, "My ring . . . It's gone!"

"You sure you didn't leave it at the house?" Marcus asked.

"You lost the ring?" Kate said, moving closer.

"I don't know . . . Let me think." Rebecca held up her hand. "Okay, I wore it at the restaurant last night."

"I remember seeing it on your hand. And it was there when we had coffee after we got back home," Kate added.

A look of relief spread across Rebecca's face. "I remember now. I took it off when we did the dishes. It's in that little dish next to the sink."

Marcus exhaled as if he had been holding his breath. "You scared me to death!"

Chapter Five

With the men gone, Kate and Rebecca had the afternoon to themselves. It was a rare luxury to spend the day with her daughter, one that Kate wasn't about to take for granted. They headed to the Country Diner for lunch. It was another warm, sunny day, so they had decided to take the convertible instead of Kate's Honda. They drove down the streets of Copper Mill with the top down, in no particular hurry. People were in their yards, drinking cider in their lawn chairs, playing catch with their children, or raking leaves and burning them in small piles along the gutters.

"I've never seen anyone do that," Rebecca remarked, pointing to the burning leaves. She turned her head to watch as residents stood guard over the piles, rakes in hand.

Kate gazed ahead. She couldn't stop thinking about Marcus' odd behavior the night before. If it had anything to do with those two men, what could they possibly have wanted with Marcus so many miles from home? If only she could talk with Livvy about the situation, but considering Livvy's current state of mind, she didn't think that would be such a good idea. Maybe she could do a little digging on the Internet instead, though she wasn't exactly sure what she would be looking for. And spending quality time with Rebecca was her first priority.

They turned onto Smith Street and pulled into a parking spot in front of the Country Diner. Located directly across from the Town Green, the restaurant was a gathering place for locals, especially on Sundays. People could set their clocks by when each round of after-church guests came through the door. The Episcopalians were always the first to arrive after early service, usually around nine forty. The Baptists were next, generally swooping in at ten fifteen, with the Presbyterians arriving shortly after them. The folks from Faith Briar were the last brunch crowd of the day, since their service ended around noon. Kate and Paul were often among the clientele, unless there was a special event or a potluck going on at the church. That afternoon, the restaurant was hopping with customers, though it was later than Kate's usual arrival time. The scent of barbecue and Reuben sandwiches filled the air.

Loretta Sweet, the owner of the diner, was standing behind the counter. Her gray hair was caught up in a net, and dark circles ringed her eyes.

"You a single woman today, Kate?" Loretta smiled at Kate.

"I guess so," Kate said. "Paul and some of the men

from the church left for a camping trip in the Smokies this morning, and I'm enjoying the day with my daughter Rebecca, who came all the way from New York City to see her lowly old mom." Kate put her arm around Rebecca and squeezed her shoulders tight.

"Mom! Are you kidding? I'm so happy to be here with you!"

Loretta gave a little snort, then said, "Well, ladies, enjoy your day together. LuAnne'll be right out if you want to take that empty booth over there." She pointed to the blue vinyl booths, with matching Formica tabletops, next to the plate-glass window that looked out onto Smith Street.

Kate grabbed a couple of menus from the side pocket at the counter, then she and Rebecca made their way to the booth. Along the way, Kate greeted several acquaintances who were eating lunch and exchanged pleasantries.

Rebecca slid into the booth, and Kate handed a menu to Rebecca as she took her own seat. They read in silence for a few minutes. Finally Rebecca closed her menu and placed it at the end of the table.

"I'm starving," she said, smiling into her mother's eyes, a look of contentment on her face. "It *is* good to be here . . . ," she said, "with you."

Kate reached over and patted her hand. "And it's good to have you here." A realization of how much she missed her daughter came over her, and she swallowed back the emotion.

"What is it?" Rebecca asked.

"It's just nice to spend some time together," Kate huskily replied. "Life goes by so quickly."

They paused in comfortable silence and turned their attention to the beautiful day beyond the plate-glass window. Cars rambled along at a leisurely pace up and down the street, and families set up Sunday picnics across the way on the Town Green.

"So, tell me more about what's happening with you." Kate finally broke the silence.

"What's to tell? You pretty much know everything." Rebecca tapped her chin. "Of course, there's always more I could say about Marcus . . ." She blushed.

"So you really love him?" The image of Rebecca smiling at Eli Weston flittered through Kate's mind. The two certainly seemed attracted to each other, and she wondered what Rebecca thought about it.

Rebecca shrugged. "How did you know that you really loved Daddy?"

Kate thought for a moment before answering. "I couldn't imagine life without him," she said simply. "He brought out the best in me, made me feel like I could do anything. And I respected his faith; he had such an infectious love for God."

Rebecca looked away, her face pinched as she squinted into the distance. Kate held her tongue, hoping her daughter would eventually confide in her. She always did in her own time.

"Did you and Daddy always get along perfectly?"

Kate laughed. "I remember some pretty good arguments. He can be so stubborn!" She paused. "Why? Do you and Marcus argue a lot?"

Rebecca shook her head. "No, not really. Though he can be moody sometimes. I don't always know why either. He doesn't often tell me what's going on in his mind. I'm sure it was hard on him not having his dad around when he was a kid."

Kate nodded. "I'm sure it was. How old was he when his parents divorced?"

"Like thirteen?"

"A hard age. Especially for boys. Does he talk about it much?"

Rebecca shook her head. "He doesn't like to dwell on it."

"There are good things about being that way, I suppose," Kate said. "It keeps you living in the moment, I'm sure. But if he hasn't acknowledged the hard times in his life, I wonder if the hurt manifests itself in other ways."

"What do you mean?"

"Oh, nothing in particular," Kate said. "Just that sometimes people who've gone through hardships seem okay until something traumatic happens, and then . . ."

Kate realized that Rebecca seemed tense about the turn the conversation had taken. The girl leaned across the table, worry filling her eyes. Kate touched her hand. "I'm not talking about Marcus. I'm just talking."

Kate paused, and her gaze drifted out the window, where a slow-moving car came to a stop next to the convertible. She scooted over in the booth to get a better look.

"What is it?" Rebecca asked, following her mother's gaze. "Who in the world is that?"

Kate could see two dark-haired men in the car, though she couldn't see their faces. The driver pulled an older-model, blue Cadillac El Dorado into a parking space in front of the diner, and the two got out. Kate strained to see their faces, and when they turned toward the diner, her pulse quickened. Rebecca gasped, and Kate knew she was thinking the same thing: these were the same two men they'd seen at the Bristol the night before, the ones Marcus had been so eager to get away from. The taller of the two glanced quickly up and down the street, then the men walked in separate directions alongside the convertible. The top of the convertible was down since it was such a gorgeous day. The men stood over it for several minutes. Kate could see that they were in a heated discussion.

"What are they doing?" Rebecca said. "Should we go talk to them? Did the little one just open the glove compartment?"

Kate had glanced at Rebecca, so she'd missed seeing whether he'd opened the compartment.

"We should call the police," Rebecca said.

"If they took something, we will," Kate said, trying to still the beating in her chest.

The men returned to their car and backed slowly out of the parking space. Rebecca shot to her feet.

"I'm going to see if they took anything." Then she disappeared out the door. The men had driven away and were now out of sight. Rebecca came back a few minutes later.

"Nothing seems to be missing." She shrugged her shoulders and slumped back into the booth. "I don't get it," she said, meeting her mother's gaze. "What do those men want? I know you saw how Marcus flipped out last night. It was so weird."

"I wanted to talk to you about that," Kate began, "but I wasn't sure what to say. Is Marcus in some kind of trouble?"

"I can't imagine. He doesn't even go over the speed limit! He's so particular. And to be honest..." Her words fell away as LuAnne Matthews appeared from the back, bearing two glasses of water that she set on the table. The heavyset, redheaded waitress was winded and stood there a moment while she caught her breath.

"Sorry about the wait, ladies!" she said at last in her bubbly way. Freckles danced across her ruddy nose and cheeks. "I had to run to the store for more hamburger meat." Then the waitress stepped back and eyed Rebecca. "You're Kate's youngest, right?" she asked, offering a hand.

Rebecca shook hands with her. "Yes, ma'am. I'm Rebecca. All the way from New York City."

"I heard you were in town on a surprise visit."

"You heard?" Rebecca asked wide-eyed.

"Small towns, honey," LuAnne explained. "Everyone knows everyone else's business."

LuAnne fingered the jeweled eyeglass holder that she

always wore around her neck. "Now, have you two figured out what you're in the mood for?"

"I'd like the pulled-pork sandwich," Rebecca said. "And a dinner salad with a Coke."

LuAnne busily wrote the order on her pad. Then she looked at Kate.

"I'll take a Reuben with Thousand Island dressing on the side."

"Okeydoke," LuAnne said and moved to the next booth.

After LuAnne returned to the kitchen, Kate tried to recall what she and Rebecca had been discussing. "You were talking about Marcus?" she prompted.

"Yeah. This trip was so unlike Marcus. He isn't usually such an impulsive person. I'd hoped he might pop the question, that maybe that was the reason for him being so jumpy. He doesn't usually act that way. But now I don't know . . ."

There was such anguish in Rebecca's expression that Kate's heart went out to her. "So, he's never been in trouble before?" Kate ventured.

Rebecca shook her head. "No. His dad was in some kind of trouble, but I don't know what, really. Then he started the moving company with Marcus' older brothers and sister."

LuAnne slipped their plates in front of them.

"Did Marcus want to join the family business?" Kate wanted to steer the conversation to a lighter topic for Rebecca's sake.

"Not really. Marcus wanted to leave home for the big city, try to make it as an actor . . . same old story."

"Yes, I think I know a girl like that," Kate teased.

"By the way, did I tell you I got a callback?" Rebecca said.

"Callback?"

"You know, Mom. When you audition for a part, and the director wants you to come back for another audition."

"Oh! That's so exciting! Is it a play I'd know?"

"No, I don't think so," Rebecca said, then her eyes clouded.

"What is it?" Kate asked.

"Oh,"—Rebecca waved a dismissive hand—"it's nothing."

"Is it about the play?"

"It's about . . . well, there are a lot of shows that . . . I mean, just look at *Grease* or even—"

"What are you trying to say, honey?" Kate leaned closer so she could speak in a quieter tone. "That the content of this show is something I might not approve of?"

Rebecca shrugged. "There are elements of good and bad in *every* show, Mom. That's called a plot, you know?"

They'd had this conversation countless times before. Or at least conversations like it, about what to do when less-than-stellar roles came knocking. It had been one of Kate's biggest objections to Rebecca pursuing this dream to be an actress.

She waited for her daughter to go on. The last thing she wanted to do was start an argument.

Rebecca tucked her blonde hair behind her ears and said, "It's a new play. Very off-, off-Broadway. I haven't gotten as many auditions as I'd like, and to get a callback . . ."

Kate knew she was hedging.

"Well . . . it's about this . . . brothel." Rebecca said the last word under her breath.

"Brothel?" When Kate realized she'd raised her voice, she lowered it to a harsh whisper. "So, you're trying out for the part of a—?"

"No, Mom!" Rebecca snapped. "If I got the part, I'd be the . . . madam."

Kate felt the blood rush to her face.

"I know it's questionable, but I just want to act so bad, Mom," Rebecca continued, as if she could read her mother's thoughts. "If this is all there is right now—"

"Oh, Rebecca. Are you sure you're not just making excuses? I think you should take up whatever career you're gifted for. And you *are* an incredibly gifted actor and singer. But in every career, there are always opportunities to make good and bad choices. It's up to you, honey, to make the right decision. I just want you to be sure that following through with this role is the right thing to do."

Tears filled Rebecca's eyes and rolled down her cheeks, causing her mascara to run. "I'm not doing anything bad, Mom. I just . . ." She shrugged again and sighed. "I shouldn't have told you."

"Rebecca," Kate began.

"I am an adult, you know!" But even as she said the words, Rebecca couldn't have sounded more like a child.

"I know. And I will trust you to do what's best." Kate took a bite of her Reuben, giving a much-needed break to the conversation. As she glanced out the window, she thought of Marcus and those strange men. She prayed silently that they had no ill intentions toward Rebecca. Her daughter wasn't the savvy sophisticate she pretended to be. She was still a girl from Texas, and she was easier prey than Kate wanted to admit.

Chapter Six

After lunch, Kate and Rebecca decided to take a fall drive, as much to calm their nerves as to enjoy the day.

The crisp, beautiful day seemed to improve Rebecca's outlook. Kate smiled to herself: that had been the way it always was with her youngest. Rebecca didn't know how to stay angry. Her good-hearted nature would take over, and not long after a heated argument, she'd be laughing and enjoying life again. It was one of the things Kate liked most about her—that she didn't mope and fret. Melissa, Kate's eldest daughter, could be that way—a bit indignant until she received the apology she felt she deserved.

As they drove in silence, Kate continued to worry about Rebecca's life in New York; she just couldn't help it. There were so many ways a young, naive girl could get herself into trouble. Kate worried more about the spiritual decay that took place in the soul of a person in that kind of profession, with the constant tugging to accept more and more questionable material, to socialize with people who could lead a young woman like Rebecca down the wrong path.

Kate understood that it must be tempting for Rebecca to accept a role she wouldn't even consider if better offers were coming in. But there had to be a line in the sand that Rebecca would never cross. There just *had* to be. And if playing a madam in a brothel wasn't it, then what was?

Kate glanced at her daughter, who seemed to be relishing the drive. Rebecca was an adult, Kate reminded herself. She would have to find her own way in the world, even if it meant taking the harder path. It was difficult for a mother to let her children make decisions on their own, especially when she thought they might get hurt. Every instinct inside her was telling her to hold them tight and keep them safe. But Kate knew most of all that safety was not something she could control, but it *was* something she could pray for. A comforting thought flooded over her. *My children, and everything I love, belong to God. I can trust him with them.*

IT WAS WELL AFTER TWO O'CLOCK by the time Kate and Rebecca arrived home. Rebecca had dozed off in the passenger's seat.

As Kate approached the house, she recognized a blue El Dorado car sitting on the left side of the driveway. It was the same car they'd seen at the diner earlier that day. But she hadn't noticed the New Jersey license plates before.

New Jersey? Kate didn't know what to make of it, but she quickly memorized the plate numbers just in case. As she pulled up to the right side of the car, two men appeared from around the side of the house and came toward her. Panic seized her as she realized that the men may have been in the house. She reached for her handbag and frantically dug around for her cell phone so she could call the police. But her handbag was so stuffed, she couldn't find it quickly enough.

Rebecca stirred in her seat when Kate began rifling through her handbag and lifted bleary eyes toward her mother. "What's going on?"

"Stay in the car, honey. Try to stay calm." As the men reached the car, she forced herself to remain cool and collected.

"Mrs. Hanlon?" one of the men said, bending over and resting his hands on the door. He was dressed in pleated slacks and a light-colored Oxford shirt.

"Yes?" Kate said, not moving her hands from the steering wheel.

"We're lookin' for someone. You mighta seen him," the man said.

Kate noted a distinct East Coast accent when he spoke.

"Who did you say you were looking for?" Rebecca asked, eyeing the man and sitting up straight in her seat. The second man was standing behind him. He was taller than his partner, and more trim, with a deep cleft chin and penetrating dark eyes. His partner was a stump of a man with black, slicked-back hair, wide features, and a flat nose. His pale eyes bored into her, and he had a peculiar way of standing with his feet spread wide yet slightly pigeon-toed.

"I didn't say." He cleared his throat, then glanced at his partner. He held out a photograph for Kate and Rebecca to look at, and Kate glanced at it as she kept one eye on the strangers.

It was a shot of a good-looking young man with a nice smile; deep dimples etched his cheeks. She heard the slight intake of Rebecca's breath at the same time she recognized the man in the photo. It was Marcus, a few years back, but those dimples were hard to mistake.

"His name's Mack Kieffer. He's from back east."

"Mack Kieffer?" Rebecca echoed. Kate heard the disbelief in her voice.

"What did he do?" Kate tried to make the question sound innocent.

"He's a friend of ours," the men said together, but their sarcastic tone gave them away.

Kate didn't know much at this point, but she could tell they were no friends of Marcus.

"Why would you be looking for him all the way out here in Tennessee? Is he missing?" Kate probed. She studied the shorter man's face. He had a nervous air about him. His right eye twitched, and the veins in his forehead bulged.

"You might say that." He said the words as if he had just decided that was his story.

Kate glanced at Rebecca, whose face had gone white.

"I'm sorry," Rebecca broke in, "but we don't know any Mack Kieffer." She shrugged, then stared ahead.

"Is there a number where we can reach you if we do happen to see him?" Kate asked. "Or should I just call the police?" She added the last question hoping it would imply the threat she meant.

The man quickly shoved the photo into his billfold. "No. That's all right. We got a tip that he might've headed this way."

"So, you're police officers?" Kate asked.

He cleared his throat, then said in a more official tone, "Uh . . . yeah. We're headin' up the investigation into Mr. Kieffer's disappearance."

"Who reported him missing?" Kate hoped she could get as much detail from them as possible so she could begin her own investigation.

"Uh, that's classified information," he mumbled. Then the other man nudged him, and he said, "Thanks for your time, ladies. We'd best be on our way."

They climbed into the ancient-looking El Dorado and quickly backed out of the driveway. Kate turned to Rebecca, who was staring hard at the dashboard. Kate could see the fear in her eyes.

"I can't believe they came to the house." Kate shot a worried look at Rebecca. "This is getting stranger by the minute."

"No kidding. I don't know what's going on,"—Rebecca met her mother's gaze—"but I'm really scared for Marcus."

WHEN KATE AND REBECCA checked the front door, they were relieved to find that it was locked. But Kate remembered the men appearing from the side of the house, so she checked the sliding-glass doors in the living room, and sure enough, they were unlocked.

"Let's check the house," Kate said nervously, feeling more and more certain that the men had broken in. She pulled a little notebook out of her pocket and jotted down the license plate number so she wouldn't forget it, then stepped inside.

After a quick perusal of the house, they agreed that nothing seemed out of place. Marcus' suitcase did look as if it'd been rummaged through, but Rebecca thought he could have left it that way.

Then she remembered her ring. She hurried to the kitchen and looked in the small glass dish on the counter where she'd left it.

"It's gone!" she said, swinging around toward her mother. "My ring is gone."

Kate frantically looked around the kitchen, opening cupboards and containers and searching every inch of floor space, hoping that Rebecca had accidentally dropped it. But the ring was nowhere in sight. "Are you sure this is where you left it?"

"I'm positive." Tears welled up in her eyes. "I distinctly remember taking it off to do the dishes last night."

At that, Kate picked up the phone and dialed the police. Deputy Skip Spencer answered on the second ring.

"Deputy Spencer here."

"Skip, this is Kate Hanlon."

"What can I do you for, Missus Hanlon?" the twenty-five-year-old deputy said in a deep voice. Kate was always amazed that someone so young would have such a voice.

"Two men broke into our house," she said, "and they stole an extremely valuable family heirloom."

Chapter Seven

Within fifteen minutes, the redheaded deputy was knocking on the Hanlons' front door. He followed Kate into the living room, where Rebecca was seated on the sofa, nervously wringing her hands together.

"You may remember my daughter, Rebecca," Kate said.

"I'm sorry to have to see you under these circumstances, Rebecca," the deputy said. "I mean, I'm happy to see you, but . . ." Skip awkwardly tipped his tan officer's hat at her and let his words drift away as he sat down in an overstuffed chair opposite her.

Kate sat down next to Rebecca, suppressing a chuckle at just how attractive her daughter was to the single men in Copper Mill.

The deputy pulled out a small notepad and pen and lifted his face to Kate. "So, tell me what happened."

Kate twisted her hands together, then reached for Rebecca's as she started talking. The girl's face was pale, and she was unusually quiet.

"We'd been gone all morning," Kate started. "First at church, and at the diner for lunch. After lunch, we took a little drive, and when we got home, two men were here."

"Can you describe them?" The deputy was busily taking notes.

Kate described the taller man with the cleft in his chin and the shorter, stocky man with the pigeon-toed stance. Then she described the blue El Dorado with the New Jersey plates. She handed Skip a slip of paper containing the plate numbers that she'd written down when she and Rebecca had first entered the house. She glanced at her daughter and realized that Rebecca was shaking her head.

"I've seen those men before," Rebecca said, looking up.

"I was just going to say that," Kate put in. "We saw those men snooping around my daughter's rental car while we were at the diner today. And last night they were at the Bristol while we were having supper. They didn't stay. They just kind of looked around the restaurant, then left."

"No," Rebecca said. "I mean I've seen them somewhere else too." She scrunched up her face in thought. Then she shook her head. "I just can't remember where."

"Could you tell if they'd been inside the house?" Skip asked.

"They walked around from the side of the house when we first pulled up," Kate said, "and the sliding-glass door in the living room was unlocked. And with the ring missing, I can only assume they were inside. It doesn't make sense, really, because they approached us so casually and said they were looking for someone."

"Do you know who?"

Kate exchanged a look with Rebecca, then nodded. "They showed us a picture of Marcus, Rebecca's boyfriend."

"But they called him by another name," Rebecca added. "They called him Mack Kieffer, but the man in the photo was definitely Marcus."

"*Hmm.*" The deputy wrote down the two names, then tapped the pen against his chin. "Did you recognize the name? Has anyone ever called him Mack that you know of?"

Rebecca shook her head. "No. Never. And when we saw the men last night . . ." Her words fell away, and Kate wasn't sure whether she was deciding exactly what to tell the officer or whether she was afraid of the implications of her revelation.

Finally Rebecca went on. "Marcus practically bolted from the table to go to the bathroom. It was like he was afraid of something. Of them."

"So, you're telling me that you think this is more than just theft?" Skip raised an eyebrow.

Rebecca shrugged. "Maybe . . . I don't know. Marcus seemed so unnerved after he saw them. I've never seen him like that before. I asked him about it when we got home last night, but he wouldn't talk. He just said he was really looking forward to leaving with my dad. Something about it being safer for me."

Her eyes searched her mother's. "What could he have meant by that?"

Kate squeezed her hand, and Rebecca closed her eyes.

Kate picked up the story from there. "The strangers did say that the man in the photo had disappeared."

"Could someone have reported the disappearance of Marcus or"—he looked back through his notes—"Mack Kieffer?" Skip looked at Rebecca. "Maybe someone didn't know you were leaving town and reported your boyfriend missing. You did come here unexpectedly, correct?" Apparently even deputies were privy to the gossip mill in small towns like Copper Mill.

"Of course," he continued, "that doesn't explain why those men called him Mack Kieffer."

"I told our boss that we were taking off, so it wouldn't have been anyone at work," Rebecca answered. "But maybe his mom had been trying to get ahold of him and got concerned."

"Do you have her number?"

Rebecca shook her head. "No. I haven't even met her yet, and I don't have any of that information." She reached for a cup of coffee that sat cooling on the table and took a tentative sip. "This just doesn't add up. Surely his mom would've called his work if she was worried."

"Oh, and the men also said they were police officers, though it was obvious they were lying," Kate remembered.

"Did they now?" That seemed to set the deputy on edge. "Were they wearing uniforms? Did they show you their badges?"

"No." Rebecca tapped her fingers on the edge of a bright red throw pillow that she was holding on her lap. "They said they were heading up the investigation into his disappearance."

Kate nodded, and Rebecca turned to her mother, fear lingering in her gaze. "But why would they call Marcus 'Mack'?"

"Maybe Marcus is his stage name," Kate offered. "Don't actors change their names all the time?"

"That's true." Rebecca paused, as if wanting to be satisfied with the explanation.

"But the good news is, Marcus is safe with Dad," Kate said, turning to the deputy. "Paul and the men left just a few hours ago. They probably aren't even set up at their campsite yet."

Skip scrolled through his notes. "What did you say the ring looks like?"

Rebecca reached for his pen and notepad and drew a picture of the sapphire-and-diamond ring.

"Thanks, Rebecca." Skip wrote a few more notes before looking up. "I'll look into that license-plate number. See if those men show up in town. Also, to cover all our bases, why don't you look around the house some more to make sure the ring wasn't just misplaced. Maybe it'll show up. In the meantime, I'll put out a description of the car and men. You might also want to try to get ahold of your husband, Missus Hanlon."

AFTER SKIP HAD LEFT, Kate dialed Paul's cell-phone number, but it immediately went to voice mail. Rebecca tried Marcus' number, but she got a recorded message as well.

"No news is good news, right?" Kate offered, but the tense expression on Rebecca's face remained.

"I can't believe Gran's ring is gone!" she moaned. "I should never have worn it."

"Don't beat yourself up," Kate assured Rebecca. "We'll

get the ring back." But even as she tried to assure her daughter, she felt a twinge of fear. If these men really did steal the ring, they weren't going to just hand it right back.

THE DEPUTY HAD BEEN GONE less than half an hour when the phone rang.

"Missus Hanlon," he began.

"Yes, Skip," Kate said, glancing at Rebecca, who had been pacing the room but was now staring at her mother.

"I ran those plates. That El Dorado was reported stolen from Atlantic City, New Jersey, two days ago."

Kate's pulse quickened at the news. "So, what does that mean?"

"It means that if you see those men again, call 911."

"Any idea who the thieves are?"

"There wasn't anything in the police report. Just that the car was taken from a casino parking lot. I've put out an APB in case they head out for the Smokies, but that doesn't seem real likely since they didn't know where your daughter's friend went."

"And there was no missing-person's report filed on Marcus?"

"No, ma'am."

Kate thanked Skip for the information, and he promised to call if there were any developments.

Kate hung up the phone, looking thoughtful, and Rebecca waited for her mother to talk.

"The car was stolen," Kate said.

"That's just great," Rebecca said. She sat down and

cradled her head in her hands. "This is so frustrating! Marcus could be in real trouble, and there isn't a thing I can do about it."

"We don't know that he's in trouble. We didn't tell the men anything about where he is. And even if they are looking for him, how could they find him in the middle of the woods?"

Rebecca shrugged, then seemed to relax. "Maybe you're right," she said.

Kate lightly touched her daughter's cheek. "The police are keeping an eye out for the car, and they have our description of the men. Surely we would have heard by now if anything had happened."

Rebecca chewed on her lower lip. "Yeah, let's hope that's the case."

"The guys are probably having a wonderful time getting to know each other and have no idea what's going on."

Chapter Eight

There was nothing quite like a day filled with vigorous activity and delicious flame-fed burgers to make a man feel content. The sun had dipped below the western hills of the Smoky Mountains a good hour earlier, and darkness had begun to take its full hold on the campsite. A faint silhouette of the treetops was barely visible against the late-September night sky, and stars were beginning to twinkle here and there.

Paul and the rest of the campers gathered around the campfire as the embers sparked and crackled. James Jenner had picked up his guitar and was strumming it quietly while the men roasted marshmallows and drank hot coffee. The glow of orange flames lit their faces.

Paul glanced at Marcus, who seemed to be enjoying himself. He was eating s'mores, a gooey campfire treat he said he'd never had before, and talking with Justin Jenner on the far side of the fire. Something the boy said made Marcus laugh.

Paul had watched Marcus throughout the day, ever conscious that this was a young man his daughter cared deeply for.

"Did anyone else hear that rustling in the brush during our hike today?" Justin Jenner asked, breaking into Paul's musings. "I think it was a bear."

"It was not!" his older brother said, pausing in his strumming. "You just *want* to see a bear."

Marcus shot Paul a worried look across the glowing fire. "Bears?"

"Yes, there are black bears in these mountains. But they're more afraid of us—"

"Than we are of them," everyone finished in unison, laughing.

"Okay, okay." Paul held up his hands. "There are a few things we can do to be safe. We need to make sure we don't leave any food out or even anything that has a scent, like that dish soap." He pointed to a green bottle near the wash tub in the kitchen area. "Let's put it in the back of the van between meals. And the cooler can go there too."

Justin got up to put the items away as Paul instructed.

"I thought we were supposed to tie food up in the trees," he said when he returned to the campfire.

"That's only if you're hiking in the backcountry and don't have something handy like a van," Paul said. "Bears can smell food from a great distance, and if people start to feed them, they become a nuisance and a danger . . ."

"Great!" Justin said.

His brother rolled his eyes, and the men laughed at the boys' banter.

"So, what's the game plan for tomorrow, Paul?" Eli Weston asked.

Paul took a long sip of his hot black coffee before replying. "Newfound Gap Road and Alum Cave are first on my list." He pulled out one of the many guidebooks he'd purchased and opened it on the picnic table under the bright glow of a Coleman lantern. "We could also take Rainbow Falls Trail if we want, or we can hike the Alum Cave Trail. Says here it's 4.6 miles round-trip." He raised his head to exchange a look with Sam, who had leaned back in his camping chair, his face turned to the dark sky.

"I can handle it," Sam replied to the unspoken question. "Or you can carry me." Sam was a bit overweight and had had some heart trouble.

Paul smiled as he read on. "If we continue on to Mount LeConte, it'd be another 2.7 miles each way. It's the third highest point in the park, and there's a lodge in that spot that's supposed to be spectacular."

"That sounds cool," Justin said.

Paul glanced at Justin's brother, who seemed to be in his own world. He'd been moody all day, and Paul wondered what was going on with the young man.

"Says here," Paul read on, "that the Epsom Salts Manufacturing Company used to mine the saltpeter at Alum Cave Bluff but eventually gave up because it was too expensive. Then during the Civil War, the Confederacy used it to manufacture gunpowder."

"Gunpowder!" Justin echoed, rubbing his hands together. "Now that's educational."

"We're not going to be mining any saltpeter," Danny Jenner said with a grin.

Eli got up to stoke the fire. He poked at the blaze with a long stick to realign the burning remains, sending up a spray of sparks, then he added several split logs to the fire.

Sam asked James for the guitar. The teenager handed it over, and Sam began to strum until a familiar melody met Paul's ears. Sam sang softly, "Just a closer walk with thee. Grant it, Jesus, is my plea."

The others joined in.

Paul's gaze shifted to Marcus. He wasn't singing or even making eye contact with anyone in the circle. He looked at the ground, and Paul could see the shimmer of a tear trailing down his cheek. Paul found Marcus a fascinating study in contrasts. He could be struck with awe at the beauty of creation or, like that evening, visibly moved by a worship song. But he also seemed to be a nervous guy. Paul wondered if the young man was as cautious with Rebecca, or whether he was able to let his guard down with her and show her a part of himself that no one else saw.

Eli moved next to Marcus, as if to comfort him or at least to ask what was wrong. But Marcus grunted something, then stood and walked into the dark night. When Eli rose to follow him, Paul shook his head and motioned for him to sit back down.

Paul could sense that something was happening in the young man's heart, though he had no idea what.

"Let him go," Paul said. "Give him some time."

About fifteen minutes later, Paul went to seek the young man out. He found Marcus sitting on a rock overlooking the valley. Paul dimmed the Coleman lantern so its glare wouldn't blind him.

"Can I sit with you?" he asked.

Marcus turned toward him, and Paul could see the twist of emotion on his face. Paul took a seat beside him.

"We didn't offend you, did we?" Paul asked. "I know we aren't the best singers . . ."

Marcus shook his head and gave Paul a crooked smile. But he remained silent. His gaze was fixed on the night sky. A few tiny spots of light flickered in the distance. Coyotes howled somewhere to the east.

"What was that?" Marcus asked, lifting his head at the sound.

"Coyotes," Paul said. There was a long awkward moment of silence before he said, "Are you okay? You seemed to be having a hard time back there. Anything I can help with?"

"I seriously doubt that," Marcus said. He turned to meet Paul's gaze. He looked thoughtful yet troubled. "You all have been so . . . nice to me."

"I don't know how nice we are," Paul said. "Kind of goofy is more like it."

"No. I'm serious. I haven't always deserved that kind of kindness, you know?"

"What do you mean you haven't deserved it?" Paul rested his elbows on his knees and turned his gaze to the night sky as well, waiting for Marcus to go on.

"I've done a lot of things . . . ," he began, then paused. "I struggle with things I can't talk about," he finally said.

"We all have our struggles, our secret fears," Paul said. "That's what grace is all about."

Marcus gave him a puzzled look.

"We don't have to keep beating ourselves up when we fail," Paul explained, "because we've already been forgiven."

Marcus let out a humorless laugh. "You don't know . . ." He paused again, as if gauging his words. "If you knew some things about me . . ." He shook his head.

Paul placed a hand on the young man's back. "Whatever you've done, you have to forgive yourself too."

"That's not easy," Marcus said.

"You're telling me. I don't know what you've done, Marcus, but no matter how bad it is, God's grace and forgiveness are always available to you. The only thing he asks in return is a humble and repentant heart."

Marcus sighed. "You guys. All of you. Today. I've had such a great time."

"And that's a bad thing?"

Marcus laughed. "No. Not bad at all. I'm just not used to it. I guess I should've expected it from you. Becky's that way too." His gaze returned to the expanse. "Forgiving me, I mean. But I don't know if she could forgive me if she knew the truth about who I really am."

Chapter Nine

K ate wanted to believe that everything was fine, just as she'd assured Rebecca. And logic told her that she was right, but the uneasy feeling in the pit of her stomach told her otherwise.

When Rebecca went to get ready for bed, Kate grabbed her laptop and set it up at the kitchen table. She wanted to do more research, but didn't want to overwhelm her daughter with suspicions about Marcus, and she wasn't exactly sure where to start. The only thing she really had to go on was Marcus' name and the fact that his family owned a moving company in New Jersey.

Within a few moments, the laptop hummed to life, and she plugged the landline cord into the phone jack. Normally she did Internet research at the library, where she had access to a high-speed connection, but it was late at night, so dial-up would have to suffice. After several long minutes, she finally connected to the Internet and opened Google. Then she keyed "Marcus Kingsley" into the search engine, hoping for the sake of her daughter that something helpful would come up. But other than a couple of references to his roles in various Broadway productions, there were no matches.

Then she tried "Kingsley Moving." Still no matches. When she keyed in "New Jersey" and "Moving," that brought up plenty of moving companies, but nothing with a name that looked as if it might be the Kingsley's business.

"What are you doing?" Rebecca entered the room wearing a bathrobe and drying her hair with a towel. Her sudden appearance startled Kate.

Kate caught her breath, then said, "Well, I just couldn't get those men off my mind, or the name they called Marcus. So I'm looking for information on him, and I thought I might get some clues by researching moving companies in New Jersey."

Rebecca pulled a chair alongside her mother and gazed at the screen. "What have you found?" she asked.

"Nothing so far . . . Wait a second; I have an idea."

Rebecca looked at her mother. "Mack Kieffer?"

"Exactly." Kate nodded, then looked up at her daughter after typing in the name and waited for the page to load. "I wish I could have you around for *all* my sleuthing adventures."

Rebecca laughed. "Yes, I think we'd be a pretty good team . . . although I probably wouldn't be able to follow in your baking-while-puzzling footsteps."

"Maybe you could sing while puzzling." The two giggled, and then Kate returned her focus to the computer.

"'Mack' has to be Marcus' real name," Rebecca said as

the page continued loading. "There's no other explanation for the coincidence, right?"

Kate sat back in her chair to think.

"What I don't get," Rebecca went on, "is why he wouldn't tell me something as simple as his real name. How hard can it be to tell the person you love your real name?"

"He could have changed it," Kate pointed out.

"But still, he didn't tell me."

Two pages of results appeared on the screen. Most were local newspaper advertisements for high-school plays he had participated in, many with photographs of a younger Marcus Kingsley. Yet all of them bore the name "Mack Kieffer."

Rebecca exhaled a pent-up breath.

Next Kate typed in "Mack Kieffer" along with "Moving" and "New Jersey." This time a business popped up. Kate clicked on the link. It read "Kieffer and Sons Moving Company, West Orange, New Jersey."

Kate glanced at her daughter, then scanned the home page.

"That's them," Rebecca said. "I've seen their pictures before."

The names of the sons—Marcus' brothers—and his father, Bill, appeared under a picture of the men. Kate clicked on the Contact page and waited for it to load.

After what seemed an eternity, an address and phone number came up.

"I'm going to write this information down," Kate said. "I have a feeling we'll need it."

AFTER REBECCA EXCUSED HERSELF to go to bed, Kate yawned and thought about doing the same. But tired as she was, she wasn't ready to go to bed. First, she tried Paul's cell number again, still to no avail. No doubt he was out of signal range in the middle of the vast mountainous wilderness. Then she called Livvy. She suspected her friend would still be awake, enjoying her uninterrupted reading marathon as she often did when Danny and the boys were on one of their adventures.

"Livvy," Kate spoke in a low voice, hoping not to wake Rebecca, when Livvy picked up the phone.

"I'm so glad it's you, Kate. I've wanted to talk to you all day, but I didn't want to interrupt your time with Rebecca."

"Liv, you know you can call me anytime. What's wrong?"

"Oh, it's just James' band buddies. They've been trying to get ahold of James about the concert. I told them James would be back on Tuesday night, and they'd just have to work their plans around that. After dealing with his attitude this morning, I've had enough of this nonsense."

"I'm sorry."

"No, it's fine," Livvy said, "and I shouldn't be unloading on you. Anyway, why are you up so late? Anything wrong?"

"I need your help with something."

"Okay, fire away."

"Today, when Rebecca and I were at the diner, we saw two men snooping around her rental car. Then when we got home from an afternoon drive, they were waiting for us at the house."

"What men?"

"I'd seen them last night at the Bristol. Marcus, Rebecca's boyfriend, practically came unglued when he saw them, and he bolted for the restroom. They had East Coast accents and New Jersey license plates."

"This is sounding a little spooky."

"I know."

"What did they want?"

"They were looking for Marcus. They claimed he was missing and called him Mack Kieffer. They even had a photo of him." She paused. "The weird thing, Liv, is that I've had a strange feeling about Marcus since the moment I met him. And this just confirms that I was right."

"Wow, Kate."

"Tell me about it. And on top of that, when we searched the house after the men had gone, we discovered that the ring Rebecca inherited from her grandmother was missing."

She heard Livvy take in a sharp breath. "Do you think they knew that Rebecca is Marcus' girlfriend?"

"I'm not sure, though they never said anything about it."

"Did they say who they were?"

"No. But they tried to give the impression that they were police officers or private investigators. Rebecca said they looked familiar to her, but she couldn't place them."

"So how can I help?"

"I did a little online research this evening and discovered that Mack Kieffer is likely Marcus' real name. Is there any way you could look into his record?"

"You mean police records?"

"I know that sounds awful," Kate said. "After all, this is someone my daughter cares for deeply . . . but I just know something's terribly wrong."

"Kate, you and your sixth sense!" The women giggled, then Livvy said, "But I don't have any way to tap into official police records, though I can search the library database for newspaper articles that list his name. And newspaper articles often include police reports."

"That would be very helpful." Kate would take anything she could get at this point. "I'd focus your search on papers from back east."

"Do you know what city?"

"Marcus is from New Jersey. His family lives there and runs their moving company out of West Orange," Kate said. She felt guilty for asking the favor, and yet she had to know the truth about this young man. Her daughter deserved the truth.

"I'll look into it first thing," Livvy promised.

KATE TUGGED THE COVERS up to her shoulders and glanced at the clock. It was 1:14 Monday morning. Images of the East Coast strangers filled her thoughts. The door creaked open, and Rebecca's silhouette filled the doorway.

"Mom," she whispered. "Are you sleeping?"

"No, honey. You okay?"

"I had a bad dream."

Kate moved over in the bed and patted the empty

space next to her. Rebecca scooted to the bed and slid under the covers.

"Just like when you were little," Kate whispered. She brushed the long hair from her daughter's face.

They lay there in silence for a while, then sleep finally came for both of them, restless though it was. Kate dreamed that Rebecca was on a faraway island, though she couldn't say exactly where. Rebecca was crying inconsolably, and Kate kept calling for her in a panic but couldn't find her. Then the trees on the island grew arms and pulled Kate into a tangled embrace. She awoke, breathing hard, glad it had only been a dream.

Chapter Ten

As soon as Kate and Rebecca finished breakfast the following morning, they climbed into Kate's black Honda Accord and headed to the Copper Mill Public Library. Kate filled Rebecca in on her conversation with Livvy the previous night.

"You told her about Marcus?" Rebecca said, her voice rising.

"She's my best friend. She's not going to go telling anyone about this." Kate glanced at her daughter. "You can trust her, really."

Rebecca sighed, then stared out the window in silence the rest of the way into town.

A canopy of colorful leaves fluttered in the light breeze as they drove down Smoky Mountain Road to Main Street and pulled into the library parking lot.

When they entered the building, they spotted Livvy in her office. She was staring at a computer screen, so engrossed in her work that she didn't look up when they came in. Kate tapped her fingers on the counter, and Livvy raised her auburn head.

"Hi! I'm glad you're here." She smiled sympathetically at Rebecca. "Have you heard from Paul or Marcus?"

Kate shook her head.

Livvy signaled for them to join her behind the counter.

"See here," she began. "I found a few articles in the *Star-Ledger*, but no police reports." She clicked on a link as Kate pulled a stool alongside her. Rebecca stood behind them, reading over their shoulders.

"Here's a birth announcement for Mack Kieffer."

Kate glanced through the short blurb that was basic baby stuff—weight, time of birth, length, names of the proud parents and siblings.

"Then, see here." Livvy clicked on another link. "A few articles about some plays Marcus was in during high school."

Sure enough, the same photos they'd seen the night before of a young Marcus popped up on the screen, with the name "Mack Kieffer" appearing underneath. He'd had the role of Othello in Shakespeare's famed play and Captain von Trapp in *The Sound of Music* during his senior year of high school.

"But there's no mention of him by that name after 2003. I've looked and looked."

"That would've been right after he graduated high school," Rebecca offered. "When he left for New York."

"He must have changed his name when he moved to New York City to become an actor," Kate said. "Marcus Kingsley has to be a stage name."

"So, whoever those men are," Rebecca said, "they knew Marcus before 2003, before he became an actor."

ALL DAY, REBECCA was a nervous wreck. Kate had rarely felt so helpless. She'd prayed about it during her quiet time that morning, and yet the feeling persisted. She called the visitor center at Elkmont to see if she could get ahold of Paul that way, but the ranger informed her that he could only try to pass along her message. He warned her that if the men were out hiking in the backcountry, there was no way to know if or when the message would reach them.

Kate sighed in frustration as she hung up the phone.

"I just don't understand why those men would travel hundreds of miles to look for Marcus," Rebecca said for the umpteenth time. She was shredding a paper napkin as she sat at the kitchen table. "It's not like we aren't coming back to New York later this week. I just don't get it."

"I'm sure that when Dad and Marcus get home, Marcus will be able to clear all this up."

Rebecca's expression told Kate that she thought her mother was insane. "He lied to me, Mom."

The hurt those words put on her face sent a barb to Kate's heart.

"There's a reason he kept his real name from me, Mom, and it can't be a good one. I thought he wanted to come to Copper Mill to get to know you and Dad. But it's clear that I was wrong. He came here to run away from something bad, something he's been intentionally keeping from me."

Kate had thought the same thing, though she hadn't

wanted to admit it. It opened a Pandora's box of questions: If Marcus hadn't told Rebecca that he'd changed his name, what else had he been keeping from her? Why was he so afraid of those men at the restaurant? What did he think they would do to him? A chill snaked down her spine. She took a deep breath and managed a forced smile.

"I know, honey." She stroked Rebecca's hair, then picked up the pieces of napkin and threw them in the trash. "I wish there was something more we could do."

Just then the doorbell rang and Rebecca turned around so fast, Kate thought she might topple her chair. Kate made her way to the front door, and Rebecca trailed behind. As Kate approached the door, she could see Renee Lambert peering through the side windows. Her Chihuahua, Kisses, stuck his chin out over the edge of the seventy-something woman's designer tote and fixed his doleful gaze on Kate. Renee may have been in her seventies, but she worked hard to maintain a youthful appearance. She frequently smelled of Estée Lauder's Youth-Dew, flaunted perfectly French-manicured nails, loved dressing in pink velour warm-up suits, and near single-handedly fueled Copper Mill's gossip chain.

Kate was actually relieved to see Renee at her door instead of those scary men from New Jersey. Then she noticed Livvy Jenner and Betty Anderson standing behind Renee. Kate could hear Livvy saying, "Renee, come away from the window. You're being rude!"

"Oh no!" Kate whispered to Rebecca. "I totally forgot

about the tea party. I'll just apologize, and tell them I'll have to reschedule."

"Don't do that," Rebecca said.

Kate turned to look at her daughter. "I don't think we have time or energy for a tea party, honey."

Rebecca shrugged. "What else do we have to do? We're kind of stuck . . . at least until we can talk to Daddy."

Kate studied her daughter's face. "Are you sure?"

Rebecca nodded and gave her mother a weary smile. "I'll just go freshen up while you play hostess." She retreated to the guest room, where her large black suitcase was, and shut the door behind her while Kate reached for the door-knob. She checked her reflection in the mirror, fluffed her hair, and pinched her cheeks before opening the door.

"I am not rude!" Kate caught Renee saying in an indignant tone.

"Renee," Kate said, leaning over to give her a hug. The heavy scent of Renee's perfume filled Kate's nostrils, and she suppressed a sneeze.

Renee made her way into the foyer, and Livvy followed, whispering "You okay?" in Kate's ear as she passed.

Kate nodded, and Livvy added, "I'm glad, 'cause Renee's in one of her moods."

Kate smiled to herself. Leave it to Renee to brighten her day without even meaning to.

Then Kate hugged Betty Anderson, the forty-five-year-old bleached-blonde owner of Betty's Beauty Parlor.

"LuAnne didn't come?" Kate asked, glancing outside before closing the door.

"She had to work," Betty said.

"So, where's Rebecca?" Renee asked, gazing around the living room. "I thought I saw you two talking just a minute ago."

"She's just getting—" Kate began.

"I'm here," Rebecca said. She looked tired, but seemed to be trying her best to be upbeat. "Mrs. Lambert, you are too trendy with that pocket pooch!" She scratched the little dog's head as he licked Renee's manicured hand.

Renee's face glowed at the praise. She lowered her face to Kisses, who swiped her cheek with his tongue. Kate glanced at Livvy, who was rolling her eyes.

"Why don't y'all come in and have a seat." Kate led the way to the kitchen, and the ladies gathered around the old oak table. It was set with a white tablecloth embroidered in tiny yellow daisies along the edges. From the cupboard, she pulled out a three-tiered serving tray and some cookies she'd baked earlier.

"Sorry, I'm running a bit behind," she said to the ladies.

"We can help," Livvy said, joining her behind the counter.

Kate pulled a loaf of multigrain bread from the cupboard, then told Livvy to get the cucumbers and cream cheese from the refrigerator. She cut off the crusts while Livvy peeled cucumbers and Betty whipped the cream cheese for the delicious cucumber-and-cream-cheese sandwiches Kate usually made for her tea parties. The women had spent enough time in Kate's well-organized kitchen to know where to find what they needed. Renee

excused herself to use the powder room, but Kate suspected she was just avoiding having to help.

"How are you feeling today, Liv? Any more calls from
the band?"

"No, and I hope it stays that way. I feel much better
when I'm not reminded of my son's rebellious attitude
lately."

"I understand that. It wasn't too long ago when
Rebecca—"

"How are things coming along?" Renee interrupted,
returning to the kitchen and squeezing into the cramped
space where Livvy and Kate were working.

"Everything's going well," Kate said. "If you could pull
out the china, Renee, we'll be all set."

Renee sniffed but did as Kate directed, collecting the
cups and saucers that matched the daisy motif of the
tablecloth.

In impressive time, the women had made an assortment of tea-party delicacies ready for their consumption.

"Are these dishes new?" Livvy asked as she and Betty
took their seats.

"I found them at a flea market," Kate said. "When I
saw how perfectly they matched my tablecloth, I couldn't
resist." She moved to the stove to retrieve the kettle that
had started whistling, then poured boiling water into
the matching daisy teapot that steamed at the spout when
she filled it. After setting the teapot in the center of the
table, she took her seat.

Renee removed Kisses from her designer tote and petted his soft head as she waited for Kate to pour the tea. The dog started to squirm in her hands, so she set him on the floor. Kisses sniffed around under the table, and occasionally Kate could feel his wet nose on her leg.

"What's it like being manless for a while?" Betty asked Kate and Livvy as Kate poured the steaming liquid into one of the cups and passed it carefully to Livvy.

"Are you kidding?" Livvy said. "I've read two books since they left. And the house is so quiet . . . and clean!"

The women laughed. Kate lifted a cucumber sandwich from the tray and set it on her plate.

"How did you read two books so fast?" Renee raised a thinly plucked eyebrow. "They've only been gone since yesterday."

"They weren't long books," Livvy replied. "Only about two hundred and fifty pages each."

"There's a reason the woman became a librarian!" Betty added.

"Did you always want to be a librarian?" Rebecca asked, then took a bite of her sandwich.

Livvy tucked her short auburn hair behind an ear and set a sandwich on her plate as well. "I suppose, though not specifically. I always knew I liked reading, and I took every college literature class I could get my hands on. So I had to do something with books—write them or run a bookstore or something. Becoming a librarian just fit right in there. Sometimes you're just meant to do a certain thing."

Kate saw the look on her daughter's face and could tell that Livvy's words were just another reminder that acting was her "certain thing." Kate could see it in the wistful expression in Rebecca's eyes.

Kate sighed inwardly, knowing that some lessons weren't meant for a mother to teach.

"Kind of like how your mother was meant to make beautiful stained glass," Livvy continued.

Kate blushed. "Well, I like to do it, but I'm certainly not a professional." She thought of the unfinished window on her table.

"You're too modest," Betty said. "Have you seen your mother's work?" She turned to Rebecca.

"Yes, I have," Rebecca said. "And she's made several pieces for me over the years. My mother's extremely talented." She shot a look at Kate.

"You should see the piece she's been working on lately. It's for a big horse farm up near Pine Ridge, isn't it, Kate?" Livvy said. "It's just stunning."

"Can we see it, Mom?" Rebecca said.

"Your mother can be very secretive about her projects," Betty said.

"That's just because I don't want everyone in town knowing when I make duds," Kate said. The truth was, she wasn't in the mood to show off her work.

"Nonsense, Kate!" Renee sniffed. "We'd love to see it."

"Maybe we can take a tour of my studio later, after we've had our tea," Kate conceded.

Conversation ebbed as the women ate their sandwiches and sipped their tea. Kate glanced at Rebecca.
Her shoulders were stiff and her gaze sober. She reached
over and squeezed her daughter's hand under the table.

Renee turned to Kate and Rebecca. "And what have you
two been doing since Paul and . . . what's your boyfriend's
name?"

"Marcus," Rebecca said, forcing a smile.

Kate could see a hint of pain in Rebecca's eyes as she
said his name.

Yes, Marcus. What have you been doing since they left?

Rebecca looked to her mother helplessly. Kate took a
long sip of her tea, then decided to share their story, figur-
ing the least it could do was help her process the details.

"Well, we've had quite a time the past couple of days.
Some strange men have been nosing around lately. First at
the diner yesterday, and then they showed up at the house
later in the afternoon . . ."

Renee lifted a curious brow. "Men?"

"They were looking for Marcus," Rebecca added.
"And we think they stole my grandmother's ring."

The women gasped in horror.

"They were in your house?" Renee sat up straight.
"What is this world coming to when a place like Copper
Mill isn't safe?" She clutched a hand to her bony chest.

"I've asked myself the same thing, Renee," Kate said.

"I'm just worried about what they'd do if they found
Marcus," Rebecca added. "It's bad enough that they took
my ring."

"That's just horrible," Betty said. "Have you tried to get ahold of Marcus or Paul?"

Kate nodded. "They're out of signal range."

"Have you called the rangers' office at the park?" Renee asked.

"They took a message," Kate said, "but they couldn't guarantee when the men would get it."

"That's ridiculous!" Renee sniffed.

"If they knew it was something this serious, surely they'd send a ranger out looking for them. Didn't Paul write up some kind of itinerary?" Livvy asked.

"Now why didn't I think of that?" Kate said. "I'm sure it's on his computer in his office. Thank you, Livvy."

Kate had to admit that having her friends around her was a comfort, though she wished the phone would ring with news that Paul and Marcus were safe and that the two men had been apprehended.

When they'd finished their sandwiches and tea, Rebecca cleared off the table while the others chatted. But Kate couldn't get her mind off Marcus. If the strangers knew Marcus before 2003, she decided, then it was reasonable that someone in his family would know them too. She decided that after she called the ranger station again, she would call the number for Kieffer and Sons Moving Company.

"Kate?" Renee leaned toward her, making eye contact. "Earth to Kate!"

"Sorry. I must have been daydreaming," Kate said, shaking her head. "What was it you asked me?"

Before Renee could repeat the question, the phone rang. Sam Gorman's frantic voice was on the other end of the line.

"Sam?" she said, her eyes meeting the others in the room.

"Kate, I don't know how to tell you this but . . ." He paused and took a deep breath.

Kate could hear the hesitation in his voice. Her heart hammered in her chest.

"Paul and Marcus are missing."

Chapter Eleven

Kate felt numb as she listened to Sam. *Paul was missing?* She couldn't seem to wrap her mind around those words.

"We've looked for them, Kate, but it's getting dark, and we'll risk losing others in the group if we keep looking."

"Sam, I don't understand," Kate said. She glanced at Rebecca, whose eyes were filled with terror. "What do you mean *missing?*"

"I mean that Marcus took off, and Paul went to go find him. That was two hours ago. We hiked up to where Paul told us he was heading, but there was no sign of them. I don't want to alarm you, but we already called search and rescue."

"Search and rescue?" Kate repeated. Rebecca came alongside her.

"They'll start looking at first light tomorrow. I'm so sorry!"

"It's not your fault, Sam."

Paul was missing. It couldn't be her Paul, she thought. He was an Eagle Scout. He knew everything there was to know about survival. Surely he wouldn't have gotten lost or intentionally deserted the group. It didn't make any sense.

Fear filled her along with the realization that this was all too real. She reached for her daughter's hand, glad that Rebecca was here with her at that moment. She took a deep breath and asked God to keep Paul safe.

"We'll come right away," she said.

"They're setting up search headquarters outside of Gatlinburg," Sam said. "We'll meet you at the Sugarlands Visitor Center."

"I'LL COME WITH YOU," Livvy said once Kate had told everyone the news. "Do you want me to drive?"

"Uh . . . I don't know . . ." Her words trailed away with her thoughts.

There were so many things that could have happened, none of them good, especially if the strangers had anything to do with Paul and Marcus' disappearance. But Sam had said that Marcus took off, so he hadn't necessarily been abducted. Maybe he'd just wanted some time alone and wandered away from the campsite, and Paul had gone after him. It had to be a coincidence, right? She kept telling herself that, yet the queasy feeling in her stomach told her not to believe a word of it.

The truth was that even if foul play wasn't involved, there were plenty of dangers in the wilderness.

Paul or Marcus could be injured; a wild animal could have attacked them. She'd heard stories about black bears that came from miles away, enticed by the scent of a backpack full of goodies. If the group had already stopped searching because of darkness, it meant that Paul and Marcus would be spending the night in the cold. Even in the fall, temperatures in the mountains could dip below freezing. She glanced at Rebecca, her expression troubled.

"*Both* of them are missing," she said, almost in a daze.

Kate nodded.

"Kate," Livvy broke in, "I'm going to drive you and Rebecca to Gatlinburg." She left no room for argument. "But we're going to have to take your car because mine is a disaster. No time to clean it out and make room. I'll run home to pack a few things, then I'll be back here in half an hour to pick you up, okay?"

"Okay," Kate said numbly.

She glanced around at the other women in the room, their faces lined with shock and worry.

"Oh, I'm so sorry—" she began.

"Don't you dare apologize!" Betty Anderson interrupted. She reached for Kate's hand. "We'll let the others at the church know to pray." She exchanged a look with Renee, who nodded.

"Search and rescue'll find 'em," Renee assured them.

"Thank you," Kate said, grateful for Renee's encouraging words.

"You go pack. We'll stay here until you leave, just in case you need anything," Betty said.

"Thank you so much," Kate said.

She rushed to her bedroom, pulled out a suitcase, and tossed in several warm outfits. Then she thought to get her laptop. Rebecca had gone to pack a few things as well.

Kate had just set her small bag next to the front door when Rebecca joined her, carrying her bags.

"Renee and I have been thinking, Kate. Maybe we should come too," Betty suggested. She glanced over at Renee.

"You have work tomorrow," Kate reminded her, "and there will be a full search-and-rescue team out looking first thing in the morning. But it's so sweet of y'all to offer." Betty sighed and looked deep into Kate's eyes. Renee sniffed and fluttered her fingers.

"All right," Betty said. "But you call us if there's any news, okay?"

"I'll try," Kate promised.

Then Betty and Renee said their farewells, and Kate checked for any sign of Livvy. She was due back any minute.

"I have a map around here somewhere," Kate said to herself, pausing in the entryway. She headed for Paul's study and returned with the map.

"What is that?" She pointed to the extra black suitcase at Rebecca's feet.

"I thought we should bring Marcus' stuff just in case," Rebecca said. "He might need it."

Kate nodded absently and drew a ragged breath.

"Daddy's going to be okay," Rebecca said as she tucked a loose strand of hair behind her mother's ear. It was the kind of thing Kate would have done for Rebecca when she was little.

"I hope so. He's getting older," Kate said. "I don't know if he can handle something like this."

"He's strong," Rebecca said. "Unfortunately, I'm not so sure about Marcus. He doesn't know a thing about camping or surviving in the wilderness."

Thoughts of Paul or Marcus face-to-face with a bear or a rattler played in Technicolor through Kate's mind, edging her worry up several notches, but she kept her thoughts to herself and sent another prayer heavenward.

"Did Sam say what Marcus and Dad were doing? How did they get separated from everyone else?"

"He didn't give many details, sweetheart. I'm sure we'll find out when we get there."

Kate walked through the house turning out lights and checking the locks on all the doors. She rifled through her handbag twice to see if she had her credit card as well as her cell phone and charger. Finally Rebecca pulled Kate to a chair in the living room and forced her to sit for a moment and take a breath.

Moments later, Livvy's headlights shone through the entryway windows, and they went to meet her on the sidewalk.

Livvy parked her car behind the convertible in the driveway.

"I called Sheriff Roberts to fill him in," Livvy said. "He's going to take time away from the office so he can come help with the search. I spoke with Joe Tucker too, since he's familiar with the park. His Uncle Warren was part of the Civilian Conservation Corps that built the park."

Tears filled Kate's eyes. Livvy's kindness humbled her.

Rebecca lightly touched her mother's arm. "Let's go find our boys," she said.

THE LIGHTS WERE ON in the back offices at the Sugarlands
Visitor Center when the women arrived at 11:00 PM. Eli
Weston and Sam Gorman were holding vigil around a map
that lay open on a long table in the conference room that
adjoined the head ranger's office. Kate, Livvy, and an
exhausted-looking Rebecca joined them. Sam and Eli
came over to offer hugs.

"I'm so sorry about this, Kate," Sam said. "I feel
responsible."

"You had no way of knowing," Kate said. "Besides,
we're going to find them." She lifted her eyes to Eli, who
looked at her tentatively.

"Kate . . . ," he said, then just shook his head.

"You look exhausted," Kate said, giving him a hug and
squeezing his arm.

"I'm okay," he said. "We wanted to be here when you
arrived."

He glanced at Rebecca and gave her a nod. Kate noted
the blush that crept up his neck and onto his cheeks.

"And we needed to talk about search strategy for
tomorrow," Sam added.

They each took seats around the conference table.
Sam pointed at the map that was a crisscross of trails and
streams, ridges and valleys.

A man in a ranger's uniform approached the group
carrying a tray laden with steaming cups of coffee.

"This is Ranger Morton." Sam introduced the tall,
good-looking man who looked to be in his late forties.
"He's coordinating our efforts with search and rescue."

"Ranger Morton." Kate shook his hand after he set down the tray. "Thank you so much for your help."

"You'd be surprised how many adventures"—he sniffed at the word—"like this I get to participate in every year. I know this park as well as my own house. We'll find them . . . if the bears don't first."

Kate looked anxiously at Sam, who shook his head at her and smiled kindly.

"We have a picture of the men for the rescuers." Sam showed the women a photo of Marcus and Paul kneeling in front of the group under a stone arch of some kind.

"I took that today," Eli said, "under Arch Rock. The ranger cropped it, enlarged it, and printed it."

Kate touched Paul's likeness. He was smiling, looking happy to be there.

"You need to know that you ladies can't be part of the official search and rescue," the ranger informed them. "Too complicated for us to try to babysit civilians."

"But that doesn't mean we can't search on our own, right?" Kate asked.

"I guess there isn't much I can do about that. As long as you have a park pass, you have every right to hike in the woods."

"And if we happen to be hiking in close proximity to where search and rescue is looking?"

The ranger smirked in response. "I guess I can understand why you'd want to do that, but I have to warn you, it's dangerous out there. The weather can change at a moment's notice, you can encounter wild animals . . .

And if you get in the way, I have the authority to send you back to your motel."

"I understand," Kate said. She appreciated that the man had a job to do, and she in no way wanted to interfere with that. But she also knew she had to help look for Paul and Marcus. She would go crazy sitting in a motel room or at the ranger station.

"So, tell us what happened, Sam," Livvy said from across the table, drawing Kate's attention.

Kate glanced at her and wondered why Danny and the boys hadn't waited up with Eli and Sam. Then she realized that Danny had no idea Livvy had decided to come along.

"Everything was going great," Sam began. "We'd had a nice hike yesterday after we set up camp, and the group really seemed to be bonding. Marcus seemed to be enjoying himself too. Even had his first s'more last night." Sam shook his head and smiled. "I've never known anyone his age who hasn't tasted s'mores. Anyway, he was fitting right in, enjoying everyone's company, having good talks with your dad." He looked at Rebecca. "Those two seemed to be hitting it off from what I could tell."

Kate saw Rebecca bite her lower lip. She gave her arm a reassuring squeeze.

Eli picked up the story from there. He glanced kindly at Rebecca as he spoke. "Then we had a good climb to Alum Cave Bluffs today. We ate some lunch and went on to Mount LeConte. No big deal, right? But on our way back to camp, we had some trouble with an old coot who had taken up residence in one of the abandoned cabins in

the woods. When we got back to camp, it was like someone threw a switch inside Marcus. He got real nervous
and paranoid."

"What kind of trouble?" Rebecca asked. She straightened in her chair to look at Eli while she folded and
unfolded a piece of scratch paper that was on the table.

Eli ran a hand through his blond hair, sat down in the
chair next to Rebecca, then glanced up at Kate. "This
squatter was a crazy old guy. Looked like he'd been living
quite a while in that ramshackle cabin not far from the
trail. He accused us of trespassing and held a shotgun on
Marcus. That really flipped Marcus out. But nothing happened, really. The old man told us to get out, and we did."

"He held a gun on Marcus?" Kate said. "Did you call
the police?"

"We were in the middle of nowhere. Couldn't exactly
call for help . . . It was scary, for sure," Eli said, "but
Marcus really lost it when we got back to camp. It was
weird, like he was expecting the guy to come track us
down. Kept referring to him as 'Sacco,' but the guy never
told us his name."

Kate made a mental note of the name.

"Paul tried to reason with Marcus," Sam added, "but
Marcus was really jumpy. Said he needed to take a walk to
clear his head."

"We didn't think anything of it, even though we should
have because he carried his backpack with him," Eli said
to Rebecca. "If we'd known that he'd take off like that, we
would've never let him go. I'm really sorry."

"You think Marcus did this on purpose?" Rebecca asked.

Kate could hear the disbelief in her tone.

"No. I don't think he got lost on purpose, but he didn't stay nearby, and he wasn't on any of the trails." Eli shrugged. "It's hard to know what to make of it."

"What time was that?" Livvy asked. "What time did Marcus leave the campsite?"

Sam thought for a moment, then looked at Eli to see if he remembered.

"It was five thirty, maybe five forty," Eli said. "I remember I'd just finished washing up the supper dishes, and I looked at my watch. The sun was just setting. Paul said he'd go check on Marcus. After a while, we all went to look for him, and then we realized that they were both missing."

Kate shook her head, still disbelieving what had happened.

"When Paul left the campsite, he told us he was going to head south toward the Jakes Creek Trail," Sam said. "And when we got there, we found his bandanna." Sam held up the red cloth, then pointed at a spot on the map. "But who knows where he went after that. I just pray that he found Marcus." He glanced at Rebecca. "That city boy would have a rough night out there alone."

"It's obvious where we need to start," Kate said. "We need to find that squatter."

KATE COULDN'T SLEEP. She kept going over the details of the briefing in her head. There had been no mention of two strangers poking around the campsite looking for Marcus. Had Marcus simply wandered off and gotten lost, or was it more than that? Had the two men given up and gone home? Was all of this an odd coincidence? Were the men connected in some way to that squatter? When Eli described the man, he sounded nothing like either of the strangers in Copper Mill, but maybe Marcus knew him. Kate remembered that Marcus had called the man 'Sacco.' Maybe the man had been following the hikers, waiting for a chance to get Marcus alone. But that seemed unlikely, since Eli had said it looked as though the man had been living in the cabin where they'd found him. She at least had to talk to the man and see for herself.

She sent up a prayer for Paul and Marcus, then finally let herself drift off.

THE OFFICIAL SEARCH-AND-RESCUE team gathered at the Sugarlands Visitor Center at the crack of dawn the following morning. Sheriff Roberts and Joe Tucker had arrived sometime during the night, along with a handful of reporters who jotted notes as they listened in on the search officials' instructions.

The barrel-chested sheriff stood at the back of the conference room, arms crossed in front of his ample belly. Sam and Eli were at the other end of the room with several strangers in blaze-orange and black garb gathered round. Joe Tucker walked over to Kate.

"Kate, I want you to know that I'm here to help you look for Paul," he said with a nod. White tufts of hair stood out at odd angles around the crown of his head, testifying to his lack of sleep. Kate knew exactly how he felt.

"Joe, I can't tell you how much this means to me."

He waved a dismissive hand. "You'd do the same. Now," —he tugged on his angular chin and cleared his throat— "like I said, I'm pretty familiar with the park, as you mighta heard. My Uncle Warren was in the Civilian Conservation Corps when the park was being developed."

"Really?"

"Of course, Uncle Warren was based at Cades Cove, but he worked all throughout the park. Showed me a lot of it in my younger days, so I know trails that aren't on those fancy park-service maps."

Kate reached to squeeze Joe's hand, and the older man stiffened. But Kate could tell by the shimmer in his eyes that he was deeply concerned.

Rebecca came over to them, with Eli and Sam at her side.

"Search and rescue's going to look along the Jakes Creek Trail and the Cucumber Gap Trail, heading south from there," Eli said.

He pulled three walkie-talkies and fresh batteries out of a shopping bag and handed one each to Joe and Livvy before tucking his own into his backpack. "I picked these up last night in Gatlinburg. They have a pretty good range, so we can keep in contact if we need to. The ranger told me what channel they use so we can keep informed of what the officials are doing."

"I'm glad you thought of that," Kate said.

"I figured we'd split up for now," Eli went on. "Joe and Kate can come along with me and Sam to talk to that man I told you about last night. Rebecca and Livvy can trail the search-and-rescue team with Sheriff Roberts and the rest of the men from our group." He handed each person a map and a bottle of water. "Did you get something to eat?" he asked Kate and Rebecca. His eyes lingered on Rebecca.

Kate nodded, breaking his stare. "We had some cereal at the motel."

"Good. We're going to need our energy." His gaze shifted to Joe. "Are you up for this, Joe?"

Joe rose to his feet and picked up the walking stick he always carried. "If you are, young'un."

"So, I'm going with Sheriff Roberts, Mom?" Rebecca asked, then looked at Eli.

"If that's all right," he said.

Rebecca nodded. Kate could see disappointment in her eyes.

"They're going to be okay." Kate said the words to encourage herself as much as Rebecca.

"I've been so angry with Marcus," Rebecca said, "but now that he's really missing, I just want him back."

"I know," Kate whispered.

"I have to believe that he and Daddy will be okay. That by this time next week, Daddy will be back at the church, and Marcus and I will be auditioning for another play—" Then she caught her breath.

"What is it?" Kate asked.

"I need to call my boss and let her know what's going on. Maybe she can notify Marcus' family."

"Isn't it too early to call?" Kate asked.

"They're already open for breakfast." Rebecca reached into her handbag for her cell phone. "Only two bars! I'm glad I thought of it now, or I'd never have been able to call later." She dialed the number.

"Hey, Connie. This is Rebecca." She told the woman the whole story, then she paused, a frown on her face. "Are you sure?" She paused again as Connie talked. "When did that happen?" Another pause. She turned to face the wall and pressed the phone closer to her ear. "Why wouldn't Marcus have told me? No, I know you wouldn't know that. I just—" Then she turned back toward her mother, and Kate could see the cloud that had settled in her gaze. Finally Rebecca hit the END button and looked at her mother.

"What is it?" Kate asked.

"Marcus was fired right before we left New York...." Her sentence fell away. Then tears filled her eyes. "He lied to me about that too."

The hurt in her expression was unmistakable. Kate pulled her close.

"He might've been too embarrassed to tell you," Kate offered. "Maybe he—"

"No." Rebecca shook her head and pulled away. "He hasn't opened up to me once, not really. He's told me so many lies. He doesn't trust me with the truth." Then her gaze shifted around the room as she realized that the others had heard her conversation. She looked out the window and whispered, "How many other things has he lied about?"

KATE AND THE OTHERS made their way outside to begin their search for Paul and Marcus. Kate saw Livvy standing nearby and noticed the terse look on her face. She was talking to James, who towered over his mother. His arms were crossed over his chest and his jaw muscle flexed.

"I said this isn't the time for this," Kate overheard Livvy telling her son.

"Hi, James!" Kate knew how tired Livvy was of this argument, so she thought that maybe if she interrupted the conversation, it would simmer down. She placed a calming hand on Livvy's back.

"I have other commitments, Mom," James said, ignoring Kate. "I made a promise to the guys. You act like that doesn't matter!"

"I didn't say your promise doesn't matter." Livvy shook her head and glanced at Kate.

Kate felt uncomfortable standing in the middle of their discussion, but she wanted to provide moral support to her friend.

"And don't twist my words," Livvy continued. "You knew you wouldn't be back to Copper Mill until later today anyway. So I don't understand why you have to do this. Kate's husband is missing! You need to think about someone other than yourself."

"I *am* thinking about someone else. The band—"

Livvy held up a hand. "I don't want to hear another word about the band. Maybe you need to drop out of the band until you can get your priorities straight." She leaned toward her son in a way that said "You had better listen to me, or else!"

"Whatever!" he said, then stomped off toward the van, where his younger brother and father were waiting.

Livvy turned to Kate, a look of exasperation on her face. "I am so sorry, Kate."

"You don't need to be sorry. Believe me, I understand completely."

"I hate that he's being so selfish. Paul and Marcus are missing, and he's still pushing the band thing. It's just not right."

Kate looked kindly into Livvy's eyes. "There are a lot of things that aren't right about today."

Chapter Twelve

The sky was still dark, but a faint edging of orange was visible on the horizon. The fifteen or so official search-and-rescue members pulled out of the parking lot in a large van, while the searchers from Copper Mill piled into Kate's Honda and the borrowed van to follow them. Kate, Joe, Sam, and Eli headed down the Newfound Gap Road to search for the ornery old man with the shotgun.

Once everyone was settled in Kate's Honda, Eli said, "I think we need to offer up a prayer."

The men removed their hats and all heads bowed.

"Lord, we don't know where Pastor Hanlon and Marcus are," Eli prayed, "but you do. Please guide us to them. Keep them safe and encourage them wherever they are. Amen."

A chorus of amens followed, and heads lifted.

The rising sun crested the eastern ridges of the Smokies, lighting the mountains in glorious color as mist wove through the autumn treetops. Kate felt numb as she watched the sunrise. Weariness threatened to overcome her, and it was only the beginning of the first day of searching. What if they didn't find Paul or Marcus? She wondered. It was cold enough at night with all the right gear, but without a sleeping bag . . . She shivered at the thought.

Eli told them that the squatter's camp was just north of the trailhead between two spots where the path curved back in an almost full loop. When they reached the trail-head, Kate found a parking spot, and they climbed out of the car to begin the hike. A canopy of color whispered overhead as birds lent their morning song to the sky. The trail was narrow, and in some spots, barely discernable through the ferns and undergrowth. Kate was glad she'd worn good hiking shoes and had brought along a sturdy hiking stick. Many parts of the trail were quite steep, and her arthritic knee was already complaining. Joe, despite his advanced years, proved himself nimble, though he wasn't as quick as the others. Every now and then, Eli held out a hand to steady Kate.

Within the hour, they were in sight of the rundown cabin. There were many such abandoned places in the park, old homesteads that had been left behind when the park was established in the 1930s. Most had fallen to decay until the park committee decided that preserving the homes was in its historical interest. This cabin was in the dogtrot style, with a simple porchless exterior and two fireplaces. Vines grew all over it and into the windows that had long since lost their glass.

"Hello?" Eli called out.

Kate wondered how the man would react this time to the intrusion. Would he come out bearing his shotgun again, or would he simply fire without warning? Her stomach tightened.

"What do you think he would've done if Paul and Marcus came back here?" she whispered to Eli as she glanced around the place.

"Hard to tell. But it isn't likely they came back," he said. "Marcus was pretty eager to get away from the guy."

The place was littered with all manner of debris—rusted farm machinery, a pot-bellied stove, an old bed frame, as well as tin cans in a heap that Kate assumed was a sort of dumping area. An outhouse with a crescent moon cut into its door was at the back of the cabin.

Sam and Joe walked out ahead, inspecting the edges of the property.

"Paul didn't think the man was dangerous. Just a little kooky," Eli whispered.

"But he did have a gun," Kate reminded him.

"True. And anyone pointing a gun can't be trusted." He looked around the area. "Is anyone here?" he called.

"Who's out there?" a raspy voice shouted from within the dark cabin. The barrel of a shotgun appeared at the corner of one of the two front windows, and Kate froze.

"We don't mean you any harm," Eli said, lifting his hands into the air. "We just need your help." He sounded so calm, yet when Kate glanced at his hands, she could see that they were shaking.

The shotgun lifted a notch.

"Please, put the gun away, sir," Eli said, sweat beading on his brow. "You don't want to hurt anyone."

There was a moment's hesitation, and then the gun disappeared from the window. Kate exchanged looks with everyone as they waited to see what the old man would do. Sam and Joe were nearest the house. Kate hoped their presence wouldn't startle the man. Finally a greasy-looking bearded man appeared in the doorway, shotgun still to his shoulder and pointed at them.

"Whatever you sellin', I ain't buyin'," he said.

"What kind of foolishness is this?" Joe said, his tone gruff. He moved face-to-face with the man, who looked to be about his own age. "We aren't door-to-door salesmen or the IRS. We just want to ask you some questions."

The man lowered his gun a bit, then Joe grabbed the barrel and pushed it down farther.

"Put it away," he insisted.

Finally the greasy-looking man shifted the gun from his shoulder and let the barrel point to the ground. "I don't like people snoopin' around my place."

"We just have a few questions," Eli assured as he lowered his hands. "Do you remember me?"

The man looked Eli in the face and studied him. Recognition flickered for a brief moment, but then he shook his head and said, "Sorry. I ain't never seen you before."

"Yesterday afternoon, a group of us men were hiking out here, and you ran us off with your gun."

The man's body stiffened, and Kate feared he would raise his shotgun again.

"Two of the men who were with us have disappeared," Eli went on.

"Are you accusin' me of somethin'?" The man took a step toward Eli.

"No, sir," Kate said. "We just wanted to ask you if you've seen them or if you know anything about them. One was older with salt-and-pepper hair and five foot eleven. The other was in his midtwenties, hazel eyes, athletic build. He seemed to know your name."

"My name?" The man's face twisted, and his eyes squinted to tiny BBs. "What'd he say my name was?"

Kate glanced at Eli. "Sacco?" she ventured.

"My name's Rufus McGreggor!" He raised the gun again. "Like I told you, I ain't seen no one."

"Are you sure?" Kate challenged.

The man hoisted the shotgun across his chest menacingly. "I said I ain't seen 'em!" he repeated. "You got trouble hearin'? Now y'all need to scat before I make you! You understand me?"

They each took a few steps back. "Put that thing down," Joe said. "We'll go."

The man stood with his gun pointed at the group as they moved toward the trail. Despair came upon Kate like a veil. As they came to a bend in the path, she turned to glance back at the cabin. She couldn't see the man anymore and wondered if he'd gone inside or was out back. He had to know more, she thought. After all, wasn't he the reason Marcus had taken off in the first place? She had to find out the truth.

Joe, Eli, and Sam were talking quietly among themselves up ahead. "Guys?" she called to them. The three of
them turned to see what she would say. "I'm going to head
back for a few minutes."

"But, Kate," Sam began to protest.

"I'll be fine," she assured. "I need to talk to him alone.
If I'm not back in five minutes you can come get me."
Then she turned, not leaving it up for discussion.

She looked around the premises, but there was no
sign of the bearded man. She tiptoed around the side of
the cabin, then something caught her eye. A pocketknife
lay on a crude wooden table in back, alongside what
looked to be a homemade whiskey still. She approached
the table and picked up the knife, fingering its ivory handle. It was Paul's Eagle Scout knife; she would have
known it anywhere. And next to it was Paul's compass.

A deep fear settled on her at that moment. If the man
had Paul's things . . . She quickly looked around, knowing
she had to get out of there. She needed to tell Sheriff
Roberts. The authorities would have to confront this mad-
man. But when she turned to leave, she came face-to-face
with the barrel of a shotgun.

"Where did you get this?" Kate demanded, holding up
the knife.

The man's eyes shifted, and she saw fear in their
depths.

"Someone gave it to me."

"*Gave* it to you?" Kate shouted, forgetting who was
holding the shotgun. She stomped toward the man. "No

one gave this to you! You've seen him. You know where my husband is."

The man's face fell. "Your *husband*?"

"Yes," Kate said, her voice weakening. "My husband is one of the missing men. I don't care if you keep his silly knife and compass; I want him back safe. That's all I'm asking."

The man stared at her for a long moment, then finally lowered the gun and said, "I found the knife and compass on the ground after that group left. They were trespassin'!"

Kate looked at him long and hard. Somehow she knew he was telling the truth. Paul must have dropped his knife and compass. Kate's heart sank as she realized this man had no idea where Paul and Marcus were.

When she returned to the path, Sam, Eli, and Joe were almost back at the cabin.

"It took you long enough!" Joe said, the worry on his face etched in deep lines.

"What were you thinking, Kate?" Eli said. "You could have gotten yourself hurt or killed coming back by yourself!"

"I had to talk to him alone."

"What did he say?" Joe asked.

"He doesn't know where they are. I found these and thought . . ." Her voice trailed away as she held up Paul's things, then slipped them into her pocket. "I believe him when he says he doesn't know where they are." She took a deep breath and gazed at the vast forest. How would they ever find Paul and Marcus in this wilderness?

They were almost back to the road when the walkie-talkie in Eli's backpack buzzed to life.

"You there, Eli?" Sheriff Roberts' voice echoed through the air.

Eli scrambled to find the device among his supplies. Finally he pushed the TALK button and said, "Yes, sir. I'm here."

Joe, Kate, and Sam gathered around to hear.

"We found their trail!" the sheriff announced. "Paul tied a piece of first-aid tape with his name on it around a tree branch."

WHEN THE FOUR reached Elkmont, Rebecca, the Jenners, the Wilsons, and Sheriff Roberts were waiting for them. Kate could hear dogs barking in the distance, no doubt leading the way after sniffing the clothes belonging to Paul and Marcus that Sam had brought from camp.

Sheriff Roberts came up as soon as they climbed out of their vehicle. "Like I said on the radio, we found Paul's trail," he began.

"I appreciate you letting us know," Kate said.

"Knew you'd want to be with us when we find them." The word *when* wasn't lost on Kate. It lifted her hopes.

"Here's the tape Paul put around a branch." He held up the piece of first-aid tape with the handwriting Kate knew so well. "So Paul can't be that far ahead."

"Let's catch up to them, then," Kate said, hoisting her backpack into place.

"I want all of us to remain in visual contact with each

other," the sheriff instructed. "And keep calling out Paul and Marcus' names. Remember, they may be injured, heaven forbid, but that means we need to keep our ears and eyes peeled. We know that Paul was wearing jeans, a blue T-shirt, and a red-and-black plaid fleece. He was also carrying a green backpack . . ."

Kate smiled when she heard that Paul had decided to take his backpack, even though he was just looking around the perimeter of the campground for Marcus.

Her gaze moved to Rebecca, who stood with her arms crossed over her chest. Her blonde hair was tied up in a long ponytail that stuck out the back of her Bucs ball cap. Paul had a cap just like it.

"I need to tell you something, Sheriff." Kate pulled the man aside as the rest of the group set off. "I don't know if it has anything to do with Marcus' disappearance, but there were two men—"

The sheriff held up a hand. "Skip already told me," he said. "Said you filled out a police report on Sunday on two suspicious men who were looking for Marcus and likely stole a ring from your house. It's hard to say if the two incidents are related, but we're keeping it in mind. The deputy is continuing the investigation back home, and the authorities are looking for the car and the men. Unfortunately, we don't have enough evidence to help us in our current search for Paul and Marcus. But we'll keep an eye out, Kate." He gave her an encouraging smile.

Kate and the sheriff rejoined the group, and when they were within sight of the main search party, Kate,

Sam, and Joe fanned out to the farthest edge of the search perimeter, where they were just able to see Eli and Rebecca walking together at the top of the next rise. It was slow going, as the terrain was not only steep in places but was also overtaken by thick undergrowth. Kate scolded herself for forgetting her walking stick, especially with the pain from her arthritic knee. Sam Gorman helped her climb, and they stopped often to drink water and eat the protein bars they'd brought along in their backpacks. Kate noticed that Joe looked as if he could keep going all week, but Sam looked weary.

The searchers called for Paul and Marcus as dogs barked up ahead of them. The sound of helicopters overhead was a great comfort to Kate. She knew they were taking the search for Paul and Marcus seriously.

As she walked, Kate watched her step so she wouldn't trip over fallen branches or craggy rocks. At one point, Joe held up a hand and stooped down to pick up a long, straight branch off the ground. He pulled a sharp pocketknife from his pants pocket, cut off a couple small shoots that stuck out from the branch, and handed it to Kate.

"This'll help steady you," he said.

She took the stick gratefully and used it to brace herself over thick logs and around tangled debris.

They stopped to eat sandwiches at noon. The party had reached the end of the Cucumber Gap Trail, where the trail circled back. After lunch, half the searchers would take the northerly route, while the rest would remain on a southerly track into backcountry.

Kate was glad for the break. Sweat beaded on her forehead despite the cool September day, and she was winded
from all the climbing. She had expected the search to be
physically taxing, but she hadn't realized how mentally
draining it would be. Her eyes scanned every crevice; she
noted every variation of color in the landscape, hoping for
a glimpse of Paul or Marcus. She glanced at Rebecca and
Eli as they walked up to join her for lunch on a long flat
rock where many of the searchers were sitting under a
yellow and red canopy.

"I keep thinking about those men," Rebecca said.

Kate raised her head. "The ones that came to the house."

"They must have been involved in Marcus' disappearance," Eli said.

Kate turned to the husky blond, who regarded her
through tortoiseshell glasses.

"It just doesn't seem possible that they aren't involved
somehow, but I'm stumped to figure out how. What did
Sheriff Roberts say?" Eli nodded toward the sheriff, who
was conversing with Ranger Morton on the far side of the
bald, a high-altitude meadow in the midst of the forest.
Flame azaleas, whose blossoms were long gone, formed a
thick hedge along the back side of the rock formation.

"He said that no authorities from back east contacted
him about Marcus going missing," Sam said from beside
Kate, "and that if those men had anything to do with the
disappearance, there isn't enough evidence to support it."

"Did he mention if anyone reported seeing strange
men around town?" Eli inquired.

"No, but I asked him to check in with Skip Spencer again later today," Kate said.

Kate rubbed her sore knees, then rose to her feet and stretched her already aching back. She reminded herself that Paul had added miles to his exercise regimen for a good month before heading into these woods, so it was no wonder she was feeling the pain. And the altitude didn't help either.

Just then a helicopter swooped overhead before heading south. She watched it disappear over the ridge and could hear the *thwop* of its blades long after it was out of sight. The rest of the searchers stood, and one of the volunteers gathered their lunch trash.

Ranger Morton lifted the megaphone to his mouth and said, "Let's move it out, folks!"

They spread out in a large fan again, with Ranger Morton leading the official team and Sheriff Roberts taking charge of the group from Copper Mill at the farthest edges.

It was only a few minutes into the afternoon's hike that Kate noticed a cave. And just outside it, she spotted a very important piece of the puzzle: a backpack, torn to shreds. Kate had seen that backpack before. It was the one Marcus had borrowed for the trip.

Kate shouted for the rest of the searchers. While she waited for them to arrive, she discovered another important clue.

"They were here!" Kate said, excitement filling her voice when the group gathered around her a few minutes later.

Kate drew their attention to the backpack by the cave. Rebecca gasped when she saw it. Then Kate pointed to a cellophane wrapper that was tied tightly to the low branch of a nearby pine tree.

Ranger Morton untied it and flattened the packaging.

"Nature Valley granola bars?" He pushed back his brown ranger's hat and scratched his forehead.

"He marked a trail for us," Kate said as she pointed to a tree twenty yards away where another wrapper was tied.

She walked over to the second wrapper and lightly touched it. She had purchased the box of granola bars herself.

"He's telling us what direction to look in," she said. Her gaze met Eli's. "It's his way of saying he went after Marcus, and this is the way he went."

"How do you know he isn't with Marcus?" Ranger Morton asked.

"Paul would've returned to the path if he'd found him." She shrugged and looked at Sheriff Roberts. He nodded, and Kate knew he agreed with her assessment.

"Hey look at this!" another voice called from behind the circle.

It was Joe Tucker. He squatted down just inside the mouth of the cave and pointed to the dirt-and-pine-needle floor. Everyone turned to see what he was talking about. There, clearly visible in the dirt, was a bear track, and it was right alongside the mark of a hiking boot.

Chapter Thirteen

With solid evidence that Paul and Marcus had been in the area, the search took on a new sense of hope and urgency. Fear that one of the men had been injured by a bear was in the forefront of everyone's minds. Kate couldn't seem to shake the image of an injured and bleeding Marcus, and she jumped every time she saw a tree stump, imagining it was a black bear.

Rebecca must have noticed her anxiety because she was walking closer to her mother now. Kate was glad for Rebecca's comforting presence and she worried about her daughter's state of mind too.

"You okay, Kate?" It was Sam on her left. His kind face always reminded her of a sea captain, with its weathered lines and permanent squint.

"I'm doing my best, Sam."

"Paul knows how to find his way around the woods," he assured her. "And he knows what to do if he's confronted by a bear."

"But Marcus doesn't," Rebecca said from Kate's other side.

Silence followed except for the calls from the searchers, the barking of the dogs up ahead, and the occasional helicopter above them. The searchers had formed a large circle around the spot where they'd found the granola wrappers and were walking mere feet apart, searching the ground in case one or both of the men were nearby, lying in the underbrush.

The dogs had picked up their scent, and the searchers resumed their southerly route, occasionally seeing footprints along the trail.

"It's a good sign," Rebecca said to her mother, sounding more like she was trying to convince herself.

Kate lifted her gaze. "What's a good sign?"

"They're well enough to keep walking."

"Maybe . . ." Kate didn't want to give her daughter or herself false hope, but sometimes it was the only kind of hope there was.

"But we found their trail," Rebecca reminded her. "And it looks like they were still able to walk after their encounter with the bear."

The women walked in silence for a few minutes, then Rebecca spoke up again.

"Where do you think they went?" she asked. "And why are we still climbing? Daddy knows that safety is found downstream, since streams flow to rivers and rivers to dwellings, and help. But we're going uphill. I don't get it."

"Well, if the bear scared Marcus, he may have felt that safety was higher up, or he may simply have run whichever way seemed like an easier escape from a bear," Kate proposed.

"I wish we knew for sure what he was thinking," Eli said.

A signal came from Ranger Morton to halt. Everyone stopped in their tracks and waited. It was late afternoon already, and Kate felt weariness seep through her bones. Her back and knees throbbed, and her feet needed a good soaking. But she wasn't about to give up the search. She glanced up at the forest's canopy of orange and red. Dappled light filtered down, along with the occasional leaf.

What was taking so long? She glanced ahead where the lead trackers had gathered in a circle with Sheriff Roberts. She could see Ranger Morton gesturing with his hands as they debated something, so she decided to go find out what was going on.

"What's the holdup?" she asked as she approached one of the search-and-rescue members.

A burly man with a thick head of hair and an eyebrow that crossed both eyes turned to her. "Well, we're not supposed to share that kind of information with unofficial members of the search team," he said, his shoulders confident but his eyes soft.

"Please, I know it might be strange that we're following your trail so closely, but we've contributed to this search already . . ."

The man crossed his arms over his chest, and Kate sensed she'd offended him even though her statement was true. She softened her tone as she pleaded with the man. "Please, this is *my husband* we're looking for."

The man looked around cautiously, then said in a low voice, "We're now seeing only one set of prints." He pointed to the shoe marks in the undergrowth.

"What does that mean?" Kate asked. "We know that both men wear the same shoe size." Kate remembered that from their boot-shopping trip. She couldn't believe the excursion had taken place just a few days earlier. It felt like years.

The man shook his head. "They may wear the same size shoe, but they left different prints. It appears that your husband lost Marcus' trail. We don't know whose prints we're looking at here."

Kate returned to Rebecca with the disappointing news. Whose tracks were they, and why had the other tracks vanished into thin air? Had one of the men climbed a tree? Discouragement pulled on her shoulders, and she wanted to cry. But she knew that would help no one, especially not Paul and Marcus.

"We'll pick up the other trail again," Rebecca said. "It's just a hiccup."

Kate could hear in Rebecca's voice that she was trying hard to stay positive.

But the truth was that dusk was quickly approaching. The sun had begun its downward slide, and temperatures were predicted to be in the thirties overnight. If a bear hadn't gotten the men, the cold just might.

Ranger Morton motioned for everyone to circle up, and the Copper Mill searchers showed no timidity in including themselves in the group.

"It's going to be dark in another half hour," he said. "Some of the team is going to camp on the trail so they can pick up the search from here first thing tomorrow. The rest of us are going to hike to a bald not far from

Chimney Tops Trail. There's a service road there, and I've radioed for the vans to come get us."

Panic overtook Kate with the realization that they were going to leave Paul and Marcus in the woods for another night.

"Sam, we just can't leave!" she said. She could hear the fear in her voice, and when she looked at her friend, she saw the same worry in his eyes.

"Search and rescue has done this many times, Kate," he reassured her. "They have to consider our safety as well as Paul and Marcus'."

"But it's going to be cold. We have to find them!"

She gazed into the woods behind her, hoping for one tiny glimpse of a clue, but she saw nothing except the shadows cast by the setting sun.

Though every fiber within her told Kate to continue searching, she knew it was wiser to rest for the night. She followed the second group as they hiked the short distance to the bald, where two vans were waiting. She gazed into the darkening woods one last time, then sighed and climbed into the van for the drive back to get her car before heading to Gatlinburg.

Kate stared out the window as they traversed the overgrown service road that was more a faint track than a road. Hunger mixed with fear in her stomach until she felt nauseated. The sun dipped below the horizon, and darkness took its place. Kate closed her eyes, longing to feel God's presence and comfort. She wanted a sense that everything was going to be all right. But she had no such sense. At that moment, she knew nothing except that she wanted Paul at her side—and he was nowhere to be found.

KATE KNEW THAT REBECCA had experienced a roller coaster of emotions over the past two days, just as she had: joy, elation, relief, confusion, worry, anger. Kate looked over at her daughter in the seat next to her and touched her hand.

"You okay, honey?"

Rebecca lifted weary eyes. "I don't know. I just feel numb. I was hoping that we'd find Daddy and Marcus today."

Kate squeezed her hand. She felt numb too. The woods had been foreboding. It was as if the trees had swallowed Marcus and Paul. She wanted to believe that they were okay, that the next bend in the road would reveal them, yet that hadn't happened.

"As much as I was angry with Marcus," Rebecca went on, "I still care for him. I can't help it. I think about the times we spent together the past two months . . . He made me smile. He encouraged me and believed in me. Yet he lied to me, and that's been eating at me little by little."

"I wish there was something I could do," Kate said. "As a mother, I want to fix everything for you so you never feel pain. That's what every mother wants to do."

"That isn't possible, Mom," Rebecca said.

"It doesn't mean I don't want to try."

The van pulled into the Sugarlands Visitor Center parking lot, and everyone got out. Darkness had settled across the majestic landscape, covering everything with

its blanket even though it was only seven o'clock in the
evening.

Apparently news of Paul and Marcus' disappearance
had reached the local TV stations and newspapers. A van
from WVLT out of Knoxville was parked out front, and a
brunette television reporter was holding up a microphone
while Ranger Morton talked about the day's events.

Kate was in no mood to talk to any reporters and made
her way inside the visitor center. The staff at Sugarlands
had set up a meal of casseroles. The food was waiting for
them on the conference-room table with paper plates,
napkins and plastic utensils. Kate had never been so
happy to see a simple green-bean casserole in her life.
Everyone took a seat in anticipation of the meal.

Kate and Rebecca sat next to each other, and Eli took
the seat next to Rebecca. His brown eyes turned to
Rebecca. "Hungry?" he asked. His face flamed when
Rebecca looked up at him and smiled.

"I'm starving."

"You're quiet," he said.

More people took seats around the table.

Rebecca shrugged. "I suppose I am. I thought we'd
find them today."

Kate had seen how Eli had comforted her daughter,
helped her climb the sometimes difficult terrain, offered
her water and food, and encouraged her when her spirits
seemed to flag. If Eli Weston was anything, he was
sincere. The contrast with Marcus was stunning, and
Kate wondered if Rebecca saw it.

"You've gone above and beyond," Rebecca said to Eli.

The intimacy of Rebecca's tone made Kate feel as if she was intruding. She tried to concentrate on her food, but she couldn't help overhearing their words.

"Your dad has gone above and beyond for me," Eli said.

"You're close to him?" Rebecca asked.

Kate looked up as Eli handed Rebecca a casserole dish. She scooped a spoonful onto her plate, then passed it to her mother.

"As close as I've been to any man my whole life. Closer, in fact. I think of him as a . . ." Eli faltered, and Kate looked up to see his cheeks flush.

"A what?" Rebecca prompted.

"I was going to say father, but that seems awkward talking to you."

"I don't think it's awkward," Rebecca said. "I know Dad cares about people. That's one of the things I love about him."

Kate smiled at her daughter's words.

"Paul helped me when I was at a really low point in my life," Eli said. "He forgave me too. That says a lot about a man, that ability to forgive. And it wasn't just a pat on the back; he kept including me, making sure I understood his forgiveness."

By now the diners had filled their plates and were talking around the table. Sam Gorman stood at the head of the table with Joe Tucker, who was talking to Sheriff Roberts.

"If everyone can be quiet for a moment of prayer," Sam said, but no one seemed to be listening.

He looked pale and tired, and Kate wondered again if

he was up to this physical activity. The chatter around the table continued. Finally Eli put both pinky fingers in his mouth and let out a long loud whistle.

The room was instantly silent as heads turned to him. Eli's face turned beet red. "Sam here suggested we pray, and I agree. Paul and Marcus need our support tonight. I know I've been praying for them all day. Sam?" He turned the spotlight over to Sam.

"Thanks, Eli," Sam said. He bowed his head as did those seated around the long table.

"Dear Lord," he began, "this has been one of the hardest days of my life. Not knowing where Paul and Marcus are, well, Lord, it's just unbearable. But you know where they are, and you can keep them safe. Watch over them. Find a way for them to stay warm. Give us wisdom in the search tomorrow. If you could just let them walk out of the woods, well, that'd be most appreciated."

"Amens" echoed around the table, and someone said, "And thank you for the food too, Lord" to which Sam said, "Oh yeah, and the food."

When heads raised, Kate glanced at Rebecca and Eli. He was still praying, the lines of his eyes crinkled in concentration. Rebecca watched him for a long minute before he lifted his face and turned to her. She gazed into their depths before she lowered her eyes. Then Kate looked away, embarrassed by the intimacy of their gaze but warmed at the beauty of youth. It hadn't been that long ago when she and Paul had looked at each other that way.

Chapter Fourteen

Paul shivered as he lay in the soft pine needles under the shelter of a large spruce tree. The cold of the night was already seeping into his bones, even though the sun had set not more than an hour before. Every part of his body ached from the cold.

At least during the day, he'd been able to forget about the pain and the hunger that constantly ate at him as he focused his efforts on searching for Marcus. But now that he was no longer moving, he felt exhaustion flow throughout his body. And he was parched. He'd filled his canteen at a stream that crisscrossed his path, but he was worried that the water would make him sick since he hadn't been able to purify it. He thought of the iodine tablets on his dresser at home. If only he'd stuffed them in his pack!

He stretched his limbs, then pulled a metallic-looking survival blanket over himself. The blanket was essentially a sheet of thick aluminum foil that offered little heat since the sun wasn't out to warm it, but at least something was covering him. Then he pulled the backpack under his head as a makeshift pillow and curled into a ball, trying to conserve any warmth that remained.

He'd had a granola bar for his supper, but that did little to assuage the hunger in his belly. With the amount of energy he was burning during the day, he knew he'd have to mete out the food carefully and find something else to supplement the bars come daylight. Surely there were some edible plants that he could scrounge in the forest. He wondered if Marcus had any food with him.

He still couldn't comprehend what had caused Marcus to bolt the previous day. Sure, the old coot with the gun had been scary, but that crisis was long past when Marcus fled. There had to be another reason. Paul welcomed the distraction from the cold as he thought about his conversation with the young man at the campground Sunday night. Marcus had seemed so vulnerable and ready to open up about whatever it was that was eating at him. Paul prayed he would have the opportunity to have another heart-to-heart with Marcus. He saw so much potential in the young man, yet something had kept him from reaching it.

As Paul searched, he came across Marcus' shredded backpack just outside a cave, and the image of it flashed back into Paul's mind. Why hadn't Marcus come back for it after the bear had taken off? Had he been unable to get to it? Was he lying injured? Paul had left the backpack in its place, just in case Marcus decided to return to it. He didn't want to move something and confuse or maybe even scare Marcus.

It had been impossibly cold the night before. If not for Paul's ability to start a fire with a flint, he wondered if he'd have survived. He'd lain as close to the flames as he could without getting singed, while his backside had felt the cold edging toward him. He'd had to get up several times during the night to add branches to keep the fire burning.

He glanced at the spot where he'd tried to start a fire that night. This area of the woods had been too damp for him to find any kindling that would catch. He'd tried and tried, but to no avail. Dread mingled with fear for what the next several hours would bring.

The image of Kate pulling him aside to kiss him good-bye flashed into Paul's mind. How he longed to hold his bride one more time, to enjoy her soft kiss, to feel her deep love for him.

Something rustled in the brush nearby, and Paul lifted his head to see what it could be. But he couldn't make anything out. The cold night air nipped at his cheeks. The sound moved closer. He wished yet again that he'd been able to start a fire if only to keep away the wild animals.

A prayer welled up within him. He closed his eyes.

What have I gotten myself into, Lord? he began. *Maybe I was foolish to follow Marcus, and if I was, I'm sorry about that. But I . . . I mean we—Marcus and I—need your help out here. Without my compass, I feel lost. I can't imagine why I haven't found Marcus yet. I don't even know if my mind is processing rationally. Lord, you are able to bring us out of here safely. You are able to help me find that young man. I know that in my heart.* He paused for a moment, then continued, *I want to see my family again. I want to laugh with Katie—* A lump formed in his throat, and a tear streamed down his cheek.

Was this how his life was going to end? Alone in the frigid darkness of a Smoky Mountain night?

Chapter Fifteen

When Kate and the others from Copper Mill finally made it to the motel in Gatlinburg that night, the time was closing on eight o'clock. None of them seemed eager to converse. The day had been grueling, and even though they'd found some clues that might lead them to Paul and Marcus, the overall results were discouraging. Kate knew she should call Melissa and Andrew with the awful news, but she'd put it off, hoping beyond hope that there would be no need after that day's search. Now she realized that she couldn't put it off any longer.

Kate, Livvy, and Rebecca entered the dark motel room. Danny and the boys had gone on ahead to their room two doors down. Livvy had told them she'd join them in a few minutes. Kate turned on the light and set the key card on the long dresser opposite two queen-sized beds. Livvy had been searching near her boys all day, so Kate hadn't seen much of her.

"Danny and the boys need to get back to school soon, don't they?" Kate asked her friend.

Livvy's gaze shot to Kate. "Are you kidding? We can't leave now." She paused to catch her breath. "We're going to stay here until we bring Paul and Marcus home."

Kate felt glad to have such a good friend, but she was also very much aware of Livvy's current struggle. "I'm sure James is eager to get back to his band and football practice."

Livvy shook her head. "Who can think about something as trite as that when my best friend in the world is going through all of this?"

"Having you here means so much to me," Kate said, "but what about James?"

"I want him to learn what real friendship looks like," Livvy interrupted, "and the best way for him to see that is by example. Danny and I have already talked about it. We're all staying until we find the guys."

"Okay," Kate conceded, then she mouthed "Thank you."

After a moment of silence, Rebecca chimed in. "This is *so* frustrating." She had plopped onto one of the two queen-sized beds and was sitting cross-legged, fidgeting with the bedspread. "Why can't we just find them? Today I kept feeling as if we were walking right past them but not seeing them. It's maddening! And why does the sun have to set so early? We could be searching much longer if this had happened in the middle of summer."

"And the men wouldn't be in such danger of hypothermia if it'd happened then either," Kate added.

Rebecca sighed and fell back on the bed.

"Oh, sweetie. You must be beside yourself with worry about Marcus," Livvy said.

"Yes, I am," Rebecca admitted.

Kate watched her daughter. She couldn't help but wonder if Rebecca realized how attracted Eli seemed to be toward her. Did she even feel the sparks between them that had been so obvious to Kate? Rebecca was usually so flighty about such things. She didn't even realize when she was flirting. She naturally paid attention to people, and it was often misconstrued. Kate knew she'd broken more than one heart because of it.

"What worries me most is knowing how ignorant he is of things out there," Rebecca was saying. "If he was the one who met that bear, I have no idea how he could have survived it. He could already be . . ." She shook her head.

"Don't let yourself go there," Livvy said. "Don't lose hope. I still believe we're missing some vital clue, and once we figure it out, we'll find your men." She turned to Kate. "Do you know what I mean?"

"Yes, I feel the same way. Let's think this through, okay?"

"Okay . . ." Rebecca moved to the nightstand on the other side of the bed and pulled out the pad of motel stationery and a pen. "What do we know so far?"

"Well," Kate began. "Marcus left between five thirty and five forty on Monday night. Paul went after him shortly thereafter. He couldn't have been far behind him."

"So that means Marcus was intentionally trying to get away. He wasn't just out for a stroll," Rebecca said. Both women turned to her.

"What did you say?" Kate asked, things starting to click as Rebecca processed.

"If Marcus was out for a stroll, Dad would've been able to catch up with him. He knows about tracking and that sort of stuff, so Marcus must have been running away on purpose."

Beginning to connect the dots, Kate said, "So if Marcus wasn't afraid of the squatter, then maybe it did have to do with those two men. Maybe he saw them again."

Rebecca tapped the pen on her chin. "Maybe. I guess I don't feel like I know anything about Marcus right now. There have been too many surprises, and at this point, I have no idea what might motivate him to run." She shrugged.

"Do you think he's hiding from us too?" Livvy suggested.

"Well, I guess I don't know that either," Rebecca said. "But I'm sure Daddy isn't hiding from us."

"And Paul wouldn't give up unless he knew Marcus was safe," Kate said. "He knows how much you care about him."

"Yeah, but my caring about Marcus has nothing to do with whether Daddy would look for him. He'd keep searching even if Marcus was a total stranger. And lately"—her eyes shifted between Kate and Livvy—"I'm thinking that's just what Marcus is."

"That reminds me," Kate said. "We need to call Marcus' family. I meant to do it this morning, but things were just too crazy. I think we should call even if the authorities have already notified them, don't you?"

"Definitely," Rebecca said. "When my boss said she didn't feel comfortable calling Marcus' parents after she'd fired their son, I figured I'd try to call sometime today. I've been thinking about it all day," Rebecca said, "but I don't know if I can do it. I just don't have the heart to make my first conversation with them about Marcus' disappearance."

Kate could understand Rebecca's hesitation. "Would you rather I called?" she said.

Rebecca nodded. "Yeah. I'm afraid I'll break down if I try."

"I'm going to duck out of here," Livvy said, heading for the door. "You two try to get some sleep, okay?"

Kate rose to walk her outside, where the night air was cold and the stars sparkled in a velvet sky. "Take your own advice, okay?"

Livvy gave her a confused look.

"I mean get some rest!" Kate said, reaching to give her friend a hug.

When Kate returned to their room, Rebecca had pulled up Kieffer's home number they'd found on the Internet and was waiting with Kate's cell phone in hand to dial it for her mother.

"Let's hope someone's there at this hour," Kate said. She held up a hand, signaling each ring with a finger. On the third ring, she said, "Hello? Yes, is this Kieffer and Sons Moving Company?"

The person on the other end said, "Yes, ma'am. May I help you?"

"You don't know me, but I'm calling about your son, Mack."

"Oh, you mean Marcus?" The woman had a thick New Jersey accent, making his name sound more like "Mahcus." "He changed it a few years back. Said Mack

was too blue collar for a fine actor like him! Where do you
know him from?"

"I'm his girlfriend's mother," Kate said. She glanced at
Rebecca, who was chewing her thumbnail. "They also work
. . . worked together in Manhattan at the Empire State
Café. They're both actors."

"Girlfriend's mother—that's a bit of a stretch! I didn't
even know he had a girlfriend."

"And, you're Marcus' . . . ?"

The woman cleared her throat, then she said, "I'm his
big sister, MaryAnne."

"Actually, I have some bad news."

"Oh?"

"Marcus has been missing since yesterday in Smoky
Mountains National Park."

"What's he doin' out there?" she asked, raising her voice.
"Isn't that out west, like in Tennessee or North Carolina or
somethin' like that?"

"Yes, actually. He and my daughter had come out for a
visit, and he went camping with my husband and our men's
church group. He wandered off yesterday before sunset,
and we've been looking for him all day long with search and
rescue."

"Oh no." The surprise in her voice was unmistakable.

"I'm sorry to have to tell you such awful news . . . ,"
Kate said. "But we're doing everything we can to find
him."

"I can't believe this. So, do you have any idea where
he is?"

"No. I mean, kind of," Kate said. "We know what section of the park he's in, but it's a big park. Until we find him—"

"What was your name again?" MaryAnne asked.

"Kate. Kate Hanlon," she said.

"I got your number here on caller ID. Could I call you back?" the woman asked. "I've got to tell my brothers and look into flights. Where's the closest airport? One of us needs to be out there. And my mother's health isn't the best."

"There's an airport in Knoxville, I think. I'll call you if there are developments." She rubbed a hand across her forehead.

"Thanks for letting us know," MaryAnne said.

Kate said good-bye, then hung up the phone.

Rebecca stared at her mother, her eyes wide. "So?" she prompted.

"Marcus' sister said they're going to look into flights out here."

"This wasn't how I envisioned meeting Marcus' family. How did she take the news?"

"How does anyone take this kind of news? She's shocked, trying to figure out what to do. I'm sure she feels helpless."

"Just like us."

Chapter Sixteen

That night a thunderstorm blew in. At first Kate thought she might be dreaming, but when she lifted her head from her pillow and saw Rebecca's silhouette against the window that overlooked the parking lot, she knew it was real. She glanced at the clock and saw that it was 3:00 AM. Climbing from the bed, she padded over to the window and stood beside her daughter as torrents of rain fell across the landscape. Occasionally, lightning would flash and the mountains would glow, only to return to darkness a moment later. Kate went to the bedside table to flip on the radio. Kate hoped a little music would fill the tortured silence, offering a bit of distraction.

Discouragement mingled with terror as visions of Paul and Marcus in the cold, driving rain flooded her mind. The radio crackled to life.

"This weather report just in for the Gatlinburg, Greater Smoky Mountains region: Thunderstorms continuing throughout the day with temperatures dipping into the mid- to low forties. That's a thunderstorm warning for our entire listening area, folks. Repeat, a storm warn—"

Kate turned the knob to OFF. "We don't need to hear that." She climbed into her bed and prayed for Marcus and Paul as she drifted off to sleep.

AT FIVE THIRTY the following morning, Kate's cell phone rang, and she hurried to answer it. She and Rebecca hadn't been able to sleep since the storm began, so they were both up.

"Kate, it's Alan Roberts," the sheriff said in a gravelly voice.

"Yes?" She braced herself for whatever news he might have.

"I just got off the phone with Ranger Morton. He said that they refuse to allow you and your friends out today, at least not until this weather breaks. We don't want anyone getting lost or hurt. The forest . . . well, it's going to be a mess. And the closer we get to Clingmans Dome, the altitude makes getting in and out especially difficult. The streams and rivers will all be up—"

"I understand," Kate said, but she felt as if she'd been kicked in the gut. How could she sit around idly while Paul was still out there somewhere? She stared at the rain-drizzled windows. At least the lightning had stopped.

"We'll still have a considerable search crew, so don't feel like we aren't looking."

"Are you going to be staying behind too?" Kate asked.

"No. I'll be out there," he assured. "And if the rain

stops, then someone will contact those of you at the motel. We'll be in radio contact with Sugarlands."

"Should we wait there?" At least if she was at the visitor center, she would feel closer to Paul.

"If you want. It might be more comfortable at the motel, though. Either way, someone will call. In the meantime, Kate, try not to be discouraged." She could hear the firm resolve in his voice, and her eyes welled with grateful tears.

She blew out a long breath and finally managed, "Thank you, Sheriff."

Kate said good-bye, then hung up the phone.

ELI DROVE THE VAN to Sugarlands Visitor Center after their complimentary continental breakfast at the motel, with Kate following in the Honda. Joe and Sam were already there with some of the others, looking tired.

Kate had never felt so unsettled in her life. The staff at the visitor center gave her and Rebecca sympathetic looks as they paced the floor and drank coffee.

Kate was grateful she had thought to bring her laptop, since she had nothing to do but wait. She set it up on one end of the long conference table and tapped into the center's wireless service. The computer whirred to life, then Kate logged onto the Internet. She was looking through maps of the surrounding area on the park's Web site when Livvy approached and sat in the chair next to her.

"I'm trying to get a better sense of the park," she explained to Livvy. "I want to see what areas we've covered already." Kate was about to call Rebecca over to join their brainstorming but saw that she and Eli were talking in low voices at the far end of the room, so she let them alone.

Kate pointed to a spot near the north-central side of the park. "Here's Elkmont, Liv," she said. "This is where the men were camping." She drew her finger down along the trails they'd hiked the day before. "And this is where we found the cave," she said. The spot was southeast of the turn-around for the trail, not far from a mountain-fed river.

"And the footprints?" Livvy reminded her.

"Right. This is where we lost their trail," Kate went on. "See the maintenance road here?" She traced a dotted line that led to Newfound Gap Road, which bisected the park.

"They sure don't have a lot of roads in this place," Kate said. "And the whole middle of the park is . . . empty."

"That's kind of the idea," Livvy said. "To preserve nature."

"It's aggravating!" Kate complained. She laughed at how absurd she sounded, then went on. "Assuming Paul didn't find Marcus at the cave and followed him at this point on the map, what would have caused them to go two different directions?"

"If Paul lost Marcus' trail, or . . ." Livvy scooted her chair closer to the laptop. "I'm stumped," she admitted.

"Wouldn't it make sense," Kate said, "to turn east here, toward Chimney Tops Trail? Maybe that's why they split up . . . because Paul knows that the only smart way to travel when lost is downstream, and maybe he wouldn't even consider that Marcus would venture upstream. That Eagle Scout logic is engrained in him."

"I guess that makes sense," Livvy said. "But it makes things worse for our search party."

"Exactly. All I know is that if Paul were calling the shots, we would have found them by now. So we have to try to think like Marcus."

"Think, think, think," Livvy said, mostly to herself, as she closed her eyes.

Kate rubbed her temples where she could feel a headache coming on.

"Here's another thought, Liv. We're pretty sure that Marcus is running from someone, right?" She continued rubbing her temples. "The men who came to the house obviously posed a threat to Marcus. Maybe . . . maybe he doesn't want to be found. Maybe he's being purposely irrational so that he can avoid being found."

AFTER HER CONVERSATION with Livvy, Kate went outside to the covered porch. She felt that she needed to move around, release some of the tension in her body. A cold rain fell in a slanting pattern across the parking lot. The cloudy sky muted the autumn trees, which had lost some of their leaves in the night's storm, and the September wind nipped at her cheeks.

She stood for a moment, watching the rain, arms crossed to warm her, feeling unbearably lonely for Paul's company.

"You said before that my dad helped you through a hard time." Kate heard Rebecca's voice and peeked around the corner of the building to see her talking with Eli. They were sitting on a bench with their backs to Kate. Kate found it curious that they were sitting so close to each other, since it was a long bench. It made her pause. On the one hand, she didn't want to eavesdrop on a private conversation, yet she also felt compelled to hear what Eli had to say.

"What happened?" Rebecca asked, leaning forward.

The cool rain-laden air blew Rebecca's long ponytail, and Kate felt its chill through her wool sweater.

"I was engaged," Eli began. "Her name was Diedre. She was this spitfire of a woman—a lot like you. . . ."

Kate felt her heart go out to the young man. She remembered well the heartache he suffered at the loss of his fiancée.

Rebecca lightly touched his arm. "Go on."

"Well, she got really sick with cancer. There wasn't a thing the doctors could do. They tried, they really did, but by the time they found it . . ." He shook his head. "Anyway, she went through chemo and radiation treatments, but nothing worked. She was so young when she died. Man, that was a hard time to live through."

"I'm so sorry," Rebecca said.

Kate watched as Rebecca reached for his hand.

Eli lifted his face to the breeze. "We never made it to our wedding day." He turned to look at Rebecca, his eyes filled with the grief from the memory. "Life would've been so different. She died, and I was so angry with God. It wasn't fair to lose her when we hadn't even had a chance to start our life together. It just wasn't fair. And to make things worse, in the midst of my raging, I accidentally set the church on fire—"

Kate saw Rebecca nod and recalled that she had told her daughter about the fire and a little about Eli's sad tale.

"Your dad forgave me," Eli went on. "That whole amazing group of people at Faith Briar did. It was something I'd never experienced before . . . the power of forgiveness. It's a pretty wonderful thing."

"I think you're a pretty wonderful person," Rebecca said. He bent his head to her, and she leaned toward him.

Kate pulled back, embarrassed by the intimacy she'd intruded on. Yet she couldn't help but feel a touch of joy at the exchange. If she and Paul could have handpicked a man for their daughter, Eli Weston would have been the one. He was a sensitive, kind, and spiritual man who understood how to care for and respect a woman as she should be respected. Kate lowered her head at the thought of her own husband and said a prayer for a swift rescue.

Deciding that she'd eavesdropped too much already, Kate went back inside. People were milling around, talking in small groups. Some were taking catnaps in the conference room's padded chairs. She still felt too antsy to sit down, so she walked to the next room where the sound of a guitar drew her attention. James Jenner looked up when she came into the room.

"Hey, Mrs. Hanlon," he said, still strumming and moving his long fingers from chord to chord with ease. He was a stocky young man with hazel eyes like his mother and curly dark hair like his father.

Kate took a chair flanking his and listened for a while. "You're very talented," she finally said.

The young man shrugged. "I practice."

"Is this one of the songs for your band?"

He nodded, his gaze flitting to her before focusing on a distant spot. Then he moved into a fingered section of the music, playing notes instead of chords. It reminded Kate of that guitarist she used to listen to in her younger days. What was his name? . . . José Feliciano, that was it! The melody James played was sweet, not harsh like Kate had expected. She recognized the song immediately; it was a new spin on an old hymn they often sang at Faith Briar: "It Is Well with My Soul."

He started singing in his deep baritone voice. He didn't make eye contact with Kate. She was sure he'd be embarrassed if he did. She realized she didn't know James that well except for what she'd learned of him through Livvy: He was a straight-A student, played first string on the Copper Mill football team as well as basketball during the winter months and baseball come spring. Occasionally he played special music in church and helped with worship, though Kate knew that was prompted by Livvy's encouragement.

As if on cue, Rebecca entered the room, Eli at her heels, and walked directly toward the music. She began to sing with James, and his eyes grew wide. He smiled and began to play even more enthusiastically. Rebecca's harmonies were beautiful and mixed perfectly with James' deep voice.

"That was exceptional," Kate said when they finished singing.

"Yeah, thanks, James," Rebecca added. "I love that song, and it's been a while since I've been able to sing."

"You have a gorgeous voice, Rebecca," James said.

"Thanks. I've had lots of practice. You're pretty talented yourself." She paused. "I'm going to grab some water. You guys want anything?"

"No, thanks," Kate and James said in unison.

They watched Rebecca and Eli walk away, then Kate said, "How did you arrange that hymn so uniquely?"

"Me and Bill, the lead singer in my band, worked on it together."

"Really?" Kate said. "That's a gift, James. I'm very impressed. I'd love to come hear one of your concerts sometime."

He chewed on his lower lip for a moment, then said, "I wish my parents were as understanding as you are."

"What do you mean?"

He ran a hand through his hair, then leaned the guitar against the side of the chair. "They don't listen to me. Mom's been harping on me all the time."

"What about?"

"Beats me. I'm always doing something wrong, making her mad."

"Your parents love you, James," Kate said.

"Yeah, I know. But they don't trust me."

"You're still young. Trust will grow with time."

"Not soon enough for me. I suppose Mom told you everything about the whole band thing?"

Kate nodded, and James shook his head.

"She doesn't even ask me what we're all about. She just assumes we're irresponsible teenagers, out to do . . . I don't know."

"Give them time," Kate said. "You're their eldest child. Every parent learns as they go. None of us does it right the first time around."

"So, you're telling me that by the time Justin's my age, they'll have the system down pat, and he won't have to go through all this? What a rip-off."

Kate smiled at his good humor. "You're a good guy, James. Your parents know that."

"I just wish they'd listen to me." He lifted his eyes as a thought popped into his head. "Do you think you could talk to Mom and Dad about the concert on Sunday? It came up so suddenly, and the band hasn't had a chance to practice—"

"Wait a second, James. I really shouldn't get into the middle of this. It's between you and your folks. I just wanted to remind you that they believe in you and love you."

His shoulders dropped, and he nodded in reluctant agreement. "Okay. I guess I just thought maybe if you told them that it was okay with you, they'd—"

"Like I said, I can't interfere."

James nodded again, then reached for the guitar and began to strum. "Well, thanks anyway, Mrs. Hanlon." He paused, then said, "You know, I'm real sorry Pastor Hanlon and that Marcus guy are missing."

"I appreciate that, James," Kate said.

SHORTLY BEFORE TEN O'CLOCK that morning, the short-wave radio crackled to life. Kate and all of those waiting at the visitor center gathered around to hear the news. It was Sheriff Roberts' voice that came through.

"Kate, are you there?"

"Yes, sir," Kate answered, as fear and hope mingled in a strange mixture in her throat. "Have you found them?"

"No, I'm afraid not, and I've got more bad news. This storm has erased any trackable trail. We're completely blind out here."

Kate could hear the thunder booming around him, and her heart sank. She glanced at Livvy, who pursed her lips and nodded toward the computer that was still open at the far end of the conference room.

"Sheriff?" Kate ventured. "Have you looked toward the east? Livvy and I thought that perhaps Paul followed that stream toward Chimney Tops Trail."

The radio went quiet for a while, presumably as he turned to talk to the others responsible for search tactics. "It's not a bad idea," he said when he came back on.

Kate smiled up at Livvy.

"We'll get some men on it as soon as we can, but with this rain . . ." Static buzzed across the radio, and Kate's frustration rose as she waited for a clearer signal. ". . . until then . . ."

"You're cutting out," Kate said. "Until when?"

There were a few more moments of static, then the sheriff's voice returned. "Until the storm lets up, we'll be sitting tight. The stream's high, and it's too dangerous to try to cross it."

Chapter Seventeen

At just past lunchtime the rain finally tapered off to a low pattering. Kate couldn't stand waiting another minute and went in search of Joe and Sam. She found them near the water fountain and announced to no one in particular, "We have to go!"

Sam looked up at her. "The sheriff said he'd call when it was time."

Kate met his eyes. "Sam, Paul's out there. The weather is still bad, but it's improved. And I can't wait any longer." Her voice rose in intensity.

Joe nodded his bald head in agreement. "The woman's right. Let's get our supplies."

Within fifteen minutes, the borrowed van was loaded and ready to go, despite the drizzle that continued to fall. Joe had radioed the ranger and demanded directions to the search area.

"This is highly irregular," the ranger said.

"None of this is regular," Joe said. "Truth is, Ranger, we're coming, whether you like it or not. If you want to be looking for another lost party, well that's on you...."

Kate was unspeakably thankful for his determination.

There was a long silence on the other end of the radio, but the ranger finally came back on. "I'll give you our coordinates."

Everyone seemed eager to get back to the search even if it meant a day spent in the cold. Thankfully, they'd brought warm clothes and rain gear. Joe told the driver to head toward Chimney Tops Trail. He knew a path just short of the trailhead that would take them down toward the valley.

"Pull it over here," Joe instructed when they neared the section of road where a trail disappeared into the valley below. The driver looked at him as if he were insane.

"How do you propose to get down the mountain from here?" the portly man asked.

"I know a way," Joe insisted.

"But the trailhead is just yonder." The driver pointed up the road.

"Too steep for where we're going." Joe shook his head, and the man finally pulled the van against the cliff wall and stopped.

Everyone piled out, and Joe went to look down into the valley. Kate stood next to him. The grade would be treacherous, and she wondered how the old man would fare on it.

"Are you sure about this, Joe?" she asked.

"As sure as I need to be." His eyes crinkled into a smile just for her.

Once they were headed down the trail, however, she

realized she needn't have worried about Joe. He was like a mountain goat; his spry seventy-year-old body could handle far more than her own, arthritic knee and all.

Livvy followed right behind Kate, and Kate could hear her breathing heavily. But Danny was by her side, helping his wife down the rock face and the sometimes-slippery sections of loose gravel. James and Justin followed closely behind.

The rain had turned the trail to mud, making the trek particularly dangerous. The group struggled to keep from slipping and falling. Rebecca and Eli brought up the rear. Kate noticed that her daughter seemed to be more reserved with the antiques dealer since they left the visitor center. She wasn't surprised after the exchange she had witnessed. No doubt Rebecca was feeling guilty for betraying Marcus, though that didn't really make sense. It wasn't as if the man had been truthful with her. Yet Kate knew her daughter; she was as loyal as a Labrador retriever.

Shortly after they had begun their hike, a section of the gravel-and-dirt path gave way under Kate's feet, and she started falling down the slippery trail. She reached for something, anything, as the hillside moved past in a blur of brown, green, and orange. She could feel tree branches and rocks digging into her skin. Finally her hand caught on a sapling. She held on tightly as the two-inch-thick tree bent with her weight. She took a deep breath and closed her eyes as she realized what could have happened. Eli was quick to save her, helping her to stand.

"Are you all right, Kate?" he asked, his eyes filled with concern as he looked her over for injuries.

Kate laughed as her nerves eased. "I almost bought it, Eli!" Aside from being dirty, she had no cuts or broken bones from the fall,

He smiled at her and held onto her elbow. "I'll be here to make sure you don't buy it, okay?" He helped her down the rest of the incline.

Finally the trail leveled out somewhat, though they were still headed downhill. The group fanned out in a line as they moved along a distant stream that was to their left. The rain pattered on the treetops in a rhythmic sound that was almost soothing. Many of the leaves in this area had fallen so that the forest canopy was an etching of branches against a gray sky.

"Paul!" the group called. "Marcus!"

It wasn't long until they could hear the voices of the search-and-rescue team headed toward them, just at the top of the next ridgeline.

Kate was happy at the sound of their approach, and she continued to carefully scour her surroundings, looking for any sign of the men. As Ranger Morton's voice grew clearer, Kate saw something in the distance.

"What's that?" she shouted. She hurried to the item, amazed that she'd been able to see something so small in this vast wilderness. Set on the top of a boulder alongside the trail was a small orange bottle with a white cap. She studied it, then grinned. She handed it to Joe, who smiled in return.

There on the front of the prescription allergy medicine was the name "Paul Hanlon." Relief welled inside her.

"He was here!" Joe turned to the others, then held up the bottle for the rest to see.

"I think he left it for us to find," Kate said, trusting her husband would continue to leave "breadcrumbs."

Joe was looking around for any sign of where Paul might have gone, but by then the rest of the searchers had reached them. Sheriff Roberts was in the lead. He was dressed in rain gear, with a plastic cover over his hat. Joe handed him the bottle, and the sheriff turned it over in his hand before looking up at Kate.

"He always hated how the stuff made him sleepy," Kate said, smiling.

"You think he left this on purpose?" the sheriff asked.

Kate nodded. "It was sitting on top of a boulder as if he'd set it there intentionally."

"But when?" Ranger Morton moved up to inspect the item.

"The way the rain was coming down last night, it must have been recently," Kate said hopefully. "The wind would've knocked it over otherwise."

The ranger glanced around. "Maybe not. Seems pretty sheltered in here." He paused. "So, why didn't he stay here if he was so confident that we'd find it?"

"Maybe he still hasn't found Marcus," Rebecca offered.

Kate glanced at her daughter. Dark circles rimmed her eyes, and her cheeks looked hollow, sunken.

"Well, either way, we're dealing with an irrational pattern here," Ranger Morton said.

THE SEARCHERS LOOKED for signs of Paul's trail near the spot where the medicine bottle was found. They spread out fanlike and swept the area for any indication of his presence. Kate prayed they'd find two sets of prints. The thought of Marcus trying to manage on his own was frightening. She knew that Paul had the skills to help the young man survive the cold nights as well as the dangers of wild animals. Paul also knew how to find food in the wilderness. He'd taken their kids camping and hiking regularly during their growing-up years and had taught them the basics of wilderness survival.

When the film *The Adventures of the Wilderness Family* came out, he'd already been on a kick to "get back to nature," as he'd called it, though Kate managed to convince him that she'd never survive in such a rugged environment. If people had been meant to sleep on the ground, she'd said, God would have made it out of feathers.

Rebecca came alongside Kate, interrupting her musings. Her hair hung in a long ponytail from the back of her Bucs ball cap, and she wore a thick green fleece.

"I was just thinking about when Dad saw *The Adventures of the Wilderness Family*," Kate said.

Rebecca laughed, and the sound of her voice echoed into the distance.

"Do you remember how he taught us the proper way to cut down a tree? I thought for sure we'd be building a cabin in the middle of nowhere," she said. "I could just see you flagging down a bush pilot to take you to the nearest shopping mall!"

They chuckled together at the memory. Then Rebecca sighed. "I miss him, Mom."

"I do too, honey."

They grew quiet for a while as they walked and searched with their eyes. The sound of leaves crunched underfoot, and a red squirrel darted away.

"So," Kate cleared her throat, "it seems like something's going on with you and Eli . . ."

Rebecca darted a look at her mother. "Is it that obvious?"

"You seem to like each other's company."

"He's one of the nicest people I've ever met." She shrugged.

"But . . . ?"

"But I told Marcus that I love him." She kept her voice low, and Kate sensed that she didn't want the wind to carry her words to Eli's ears. "I shouldn't be attracted to another man."

"But you are." Kate had seen the way they looked at each other, the way they stood close when they talked, as if no one else was in the room. And, of course, she had overheard them talking earlier that day at the visitor center.

"I guess I just need a friend right now," Rebecca admitted. "And learning that Marcus lied to me about his name and losing his job, and then wondering why those men were looking for him . . . well . . ."

"It's shaken your confidence."

Rebecca nodded. "Absolutely. Doesn't it shake yours? I wonder if I ever knew Marcus. And Eli is so . . . sincere and kind . . . and honest."

She lifted woeful eyes to her mother and went on. "It's not fair to Marcus. I haven't had the chance to hear his explanation. Maybe this is all just a big misunderstanding." She shook her head. "Oh, who am I fooling? I'm too confused right now to even think of Eli as more than a friend, not to mention the fact that he lives here and I live in New York."

Kate patted her shoulder. "You'll figure it out, honey."

"I hope so. Sometimes I'm so mad at Marcus, but then I remember the Marcus of a few days ago, and I miss him so much."

Just then someone ahead began shouting. Kate and Rebecca glanced at each other and hurried to see what was going on.

"Kate!" Sam called, his wrinkled face turning up in a smile. "We found a print!"

Elation bubbled in Kate's heart. She moved to see where he pointed. Sure enough, there in the mud was a clear boot print.

"Not two sets?" she checked, but as the words left her mouth, Eli began shouting ahead. Kate met Sam's eye, and the two of them rushed to the young man.

"More prints!" he shouted. "And two more granola wrappers."

Kate closed her eyes in relief. She moved from one

tree to the next, following the path Paul had left as the men followed behind. There were only three wrappers, but it was enough of a sign, along with his prints, to know where he'd headed.

After examining the first set of prints, Ranger Morton and the other searchers approached Kate. "The prints are headed in two different directions," he said.

"Could Paul and Marcus have missed each other?"

"At this point, that's my only explanation, unless one of them changed direction. But we can't tell for sure," Ranger Morton replied. "What we do know is that these prints are fresh."

"So, we split up, then?" Kate asked.

The ranger nodded. "Seems we'll have to."

"This has to be Paul's track," Kate went on. "He's the only one who would tie granola wrappers to the trees. I'm going to see where it goes."

"I'll go with her," Sam, Joe, and Eli said at the same time.

Then Joe spoke again. "We aren't far from the road, and I know a thing or two about tracking." He met the ranger's eyes. "We can radio back if we find anything."

The ranger nodded his consent. Finally Sheriff Roberts said, "I'll come too."

So the five climbed toward the Appalachian Trail, east of Clingmans Dome, while Rebecca and the Jenners and the Wilsons kept up their search for Marcus with the ranger and his men.

Kate and the others had an easy time following the footprints at first, because the boots had left deep impressions in the muddy terrain. But when the path crossed a small stream, the prints disappeared. The group walked up and down the other side of the bank, then finally stopped to talk through where to go next. Kate's legs ached from walking and her arthritic knee begged for a rest. She sat on a fallen log to allow herself a reprieve.

"It looks to me like he was headed toward where the Spruce-Fir Nature Trail meets Clingmans Dome Road," Joe offered.

"Or he could've walked in the stream for a ways," Sam said. "That would account for us not being able to find footprints."

Kate thought it over. After the rain, Paul probably would have been doubly concerned for Marcus' safety. Perhaps he'd decided he couldn't find the young man on his own. If that were the case, it would have been logical that he'd have gone to the road, looking for help . . .

"How far is it to the road?" she asked Joe.

"I'd say another half mile. Not too bad."

Though the way her legs were aching, he may as well have said another six miles. She glanced at the others, who seemed as tired as she felt—especially Sam, who looked a bit pale.

"You holding up okay, Sam?" she asked.

He waved a "Don't worry about me" hand at her and stood back up.

That half mile was a steep one, with some straight climbs over rocks. Eli helped Kate up the trail. She was glad the young man was so strong.

When the group finally reached the road, they sank on a boulder alongside the roadbed. Kate's feet and legs throbbed from all the exertion.

The men sat down too. She could read the exhaustion in their bodies. Their shoulders drooped, and dark circles ringed their eyes.

Kate glanced at Eli, who was on her left. He pulled a water bottle from his pack and took a long drink. A part of her wished something more would come of the mutual attraction between him and Rebecca. Kate had such affection for him and, since this experience, a greater degree of respect too. He'd shown himself as a person of character, someone who could be trusted, someone whose faith would challenge Rebecca's. The fact that he lived in Copper Mill didn't hurt either.

"I think we've completely lost his trail," the sheriff was saying. Kate glanced at his somber face. "There were no signs of Paul after we crossed that stream, and I don't see any evidence that he was on this road."

"He could've walked along the stream for a while as Sam suggested. It wasn't more than a few inches deep." Kate had to admit that the more she thought about it, the more she realized the sheriff was probably right. Paul would have left another sign for them on the road if he had been here. When she voiced her thoughts to the group, Eli and Sheriff Roberts decided to walk in opposite directions along the roadbed, looking for just such a sign. That gave Kate the perfect opportunity to rest on a nearby boulder.

After a good half hour of walking, the men returned to

the group and confessed that they hadn't seen any signs of Paul.

Eli shook his head. "I think you're right, Kate. Your husband's gotta be in those woods."

The half-hour rest on the boulder had refreshed Kate. She felt ready to press on with the search. Rising to her feet, she said, "Then let's radio the others and head back down into the valley."

Everyone but Sam stood. Kate turned back to look at him. His face was ghostly pale, and his eyes were closed.

"Sam, are you okay?" Kate bent over to touch his forehead. He was cold and clammy.

He nodded but remained motionless.

"You're *not* okay," Kate finally said. She looked to the other men, fear rising in her throat.

Sam reached a hand to his chest and laid his palm across his heart. "Just a little . . . pain," he managed to get out.

"How long have you felt this way?" she asked, frowning.

"A couple days."

"A couple days? Oh, Sam. You need to go to a hospital."

"It's nothing . . . just some pressure." He placed his hands on the rock to brace himself to stand.

Kate looked the sheriff in the eye as worry for her friend's health grew. "Where's the nearest emergency room?" she asked.

"I think it's in Sevierville."

"Let's get an ambulance in here. We're going to the hospital," she said.

"No!" Sam protested. "We need to be here . . . for Paul."

"Paul would never forgive himself if something happened to you while we were out looking for him. You know that, Sam Gorman." She hadn't meant to scold him, and yet she couldn't help herself.

Sheriff Roberts radioed Sugarlands and ordered them to call for an ambulance immediately, giving the group's location. "An ambulance will be here any minute now, Sam," he assured, bending down to feel Sam's pulse.

"You stay looking. I'll go to the hospital with him," Joe offered. "I'm feeling a bit tired myself." He smiled at Sam. "It'll give me some time to rest." Then he turned to Kate, nodding toward Sheriff Roberts and Eli. "Besides, these two strapping young men can help you more than an old fool like me."

AFTER THE AMBULANCE left for the hospital, Kate, Eli, and Sheriff Roberts retraced their steps to the valley below. Kate realized she had underestimated how tired she really was and how difficult the walk back down would be. After less than a mile, she was feeling her age. With each step, she willed her legs to move. She was getting a headache too. They stopped to drink water and rest. Kate realized she was short of breath, and she thought of Sam speeding toward the emergency room. He'd looked so helpless strapped to that gurney as it rolled into the back of the ambulance. But she knew there was nothing wrong with her that a regimen of exercise and healthy eating wouldn't fix, so she determined to push ahead.

"It's the altitude that's making us feel winded," the sheriff said as he pointed to the mountaintop ahead. "We're at five thousand feet and climbing."

"I don't know if I can make it," Kate said.

"I can call on the radio," he offered. "See if we can get a ride to the trailhead."

Kate sighed, hating the limitations age could put on a person.

"There are a lot of people looking for him," Eli reminded her. "You don't have to be Wonder Woman."

Kate smiled at the image. "I'm hardly Wonder Woman. But I do want to find my husband. Just give me some time. I'm not about to give up now because of a silly thing like exhaustion."

Chapter Eighteen

After sitting in the cool late-afternoon sunshine, Kate began to feel better. The last thing she wanted to do was give up the search just before finding Paul and Marcus. And Paul felt so close. They could be waiting just up the road for all she knew. So while Kate rested, her companions searched the general area, and after a good forty minutes, they returned.

As she stood, the radio in Sheriff Roberts' belt buzzed. "Sheriff Roberts, come in. Over." It was Ranger Morton.

"I'm here. What do you have?"

"We found two sets of prints, and they look to be walking side by side."

The sheriff confirmed their location and told them they'd meet them at the junction of the Spruce-Fir Nature Trail and Clingmans Dome Road, then he signed off.

Kate smiled into his weary eyes. "Let's go," she said.

The remainder of the climb was challenging, but Kate managed to make it to the trailhead. It was a beautiful area of the park that had an almost medieval feel to it.

Tall, straight conifers speared the sky, their dark green foliage drooping luxuriously. Mist laced in and out of the mountains at this altitude.

They waited at the meeting spot for what felt like a long time, but there was no sign of the other searchers headed their way. The sun balanced on the tightrope of horizon beyond the western mountains. The group watched it without speaking.

Kate tried to keep her anxiety from returning with the approaching dusk and reflected if only for a moment on God's beautiful creation. But still, she felt so frustrated. Sure, these forests were huge, but with the clues Paul had left and the number of searchers scouring the terrain, she felt sure they should have found the men by now. But with the sun setting so soon, they'd have to call it a night again.

Her stomach knotted at the thought of Paul and Marcus out in the woods for a third cold night.

Just then, the radio crackled, and the ranger came on, "Sheriff, are you there? Come in. Over."

Sheriff Roberts shot a glance at Kate before pushing the TALK button. "Yes, sir. What's going on? I thought we were meeting you where the Spruce-Fir Nature Trail meets Clingmans Dome Road."

"It's taking longer than we expected," Kate heard the ranger say. "It's rough going. Lots of steep terrain."

"But no sign of Paul or Marcus?" the sheriff asked.

"No. Nothing new to report on that front. We're going to set up camp pretty quick. Hopefully it's not too muddy.

A van's going to pick you up on the Spruce-Fir Nature Trail and take you back to Sugarlands."

"All right," Sheriff Roberts said. "Over and out."

Kate sighed, discouraged that they were quitting for the night. "It feels like we're so close," she said, then lifted her gaze to Eli.

The young man reached for her hand and gave it a squeeze. "I'm sorry, Kate," he said.

Sheriff Roberts looked at Kate soberly. "It's getting dark," he said. "I think they're close; I really do. But we're just going to have to hold tight, do some of that praying you're always talking about."

The comment struck Kate like a slap in the face. He was telling her to pray? But she knew he was right. She'd let others pray, and she'd thought of God and sent up arrow-prayers to him, but she hadn't poured out her heart to him, hadn't asked him for the wisdom she so desperately needed. She'd been relying on her own strength, her own intuition to will Paul and Marcus home.

WHEN THEY ARRIVED BACK at the motel, Kate called Andrew and Melissa to update them, then called the hospital to check on Sam, since visiting hours were long past. Joe told her that Sam was doing well. He'd had a "cardiac event," as the doctors had called it, though Joe didn't know exactly what that meant.

"They said it wasn't an all-out heart attack, but they're going to keep him here for observation. In any case, he can't be out searching anymore. It's too hard on him."

"Are you coming back to the motel so you can rest?" Kate asked the seventy-year-old.

"I'm gonna wait it out here until I know Sam's out of the woods. Shouldn't be more than a few days," he said. "They have La-Z-Boy chairs in the rooms, so I'm all set. The nurse even sneaked me some pudding . . . I think she's sweet on me!"

Kate laughed, then thanked Joe for taking good care of Sam before she hung up the phone. Rebecca was in the bathroom brushing her teeth.

Kate thought about what the sheriff had said to her about praying. She knew he hadn't meant anything by it, but she'd been thinking about it all evening. She closed her eyes as weariness of soul mingled with weariness of body.

"Lord," she prayed out loud. The prayer welled up inside her. She could feel it to her very core—"I can't do this. My faith isn't strong enough, but I know you love me even if I can't feel it. So I'm going to trust you with an open hand. Our lives are yours to do with as you will. Help me not to hold on so tightly but to know that you love Paul and me far more than we can love each other. You have our best interests in mind. You deserve my trust. Please keep Paul and Marcus safe. Give them a sense of direction so they can just walk out of those woods. Give Sheriff Roberts and Ranger Morton and the other men in charge the wisdom they need."

When she opened her eyes, Rebecca was gazing at her, tears streaming down her cheeks. "Thanks, Mom," she said.

"What for?" Kate asked, puzzled.

"For being an example."

"What do you mean?" Kate patted the spot next to her on the bed, and Rebecca plopped down beside her.

"You and Dad never just told us what to do. I mean, you told us, but you also *showed* us. I appreciate that. You actually live what you believe. I guess I'd forgotten that while I'd been away from you." She shrugged, and Kate patted her hand.

"I've missed you," Rebecca added, then she chuckled to herself. "It's funny how some time in the woods can give a person perspective, but today I had a realization."

"And what was that?" Kate asked.

"I've been so hurt by Marcus' deception, and I've been wondering what I did that caused him not to trust me. But maybe he did try to tell me in his own way. There were things that he said, weird things that I didn't understand at the time, but they're beginning to make sense now."

"What kinds of things?" Kate said.

"He'd make these comments like, 'Some things are too big for forgiveness.' I'd try to probe into what he meant, asking if he was talking about something in his own past, but then he'd always clam up. Maybe he was hoping I could crack that shell open, and he was giving me an opportunity."

"But that's not your fault," Kate said.

"I know that. I just feel like I could have tried harder to draw him out. Sometimes things can be too hard to say out loud."

Kate chimed in. "I think you're right. It's scary to let people in, especially someone you care about and don't want to lose."

Rebecca went on. "But still, the clues were all there—the impromptu trip to Copper Mill, the nervous way he was acting—but I didn't start paying attention until a few days ago. He seemed eager to come here, even though we haven't even made the trek to New Jersey to meet his family. I think he was trying to get away from those men, but I wonder if he was also trying to forget about something. Maybe he wanted to forget about losing his job, but that seems small compared to whatever it is those two men are after." She paused and lifted her face in contemplation. "I wish I knew what those men want from Marcus."

"I was just thinking the same thing," Kate said. "Has Marcus said anything that might clue us in?"

"I haven't thought of anything yet," Rebecca admitted. "There has to be a good reason why those men would travel hundreds of miles in search of him. They claimed Marcus was missing, and now he *is* missing. I don't know if that's just a coincidence, but I hope it is, because if those men had anything to do with his disappearance, they could be doing all sorts of horrible things to Marcus and to Daddy. I couldn't bear the thought of that."

She lifted her eyes to Kate's, then her expression darkened. "There's something else," she said. "I know I said earlier that I couldn't think of Eli as more than a friend . . ."

"Your feelings have changed?"

"I don't know. I think so. He's such a stark contrast to

Marcus. He's an open book, warts and all, and I find that so refreshing. He told me about losing his fiancée and everything that happened after that."

"That was a difficult time for him," Kate said.

"And yet he isn't ashamed of his past. He sees it for what it was, and he's stronger because of it."

"That's what mature people do," Kate said. "They learn and grow from their mistakes."

Rebecca nodded and began to twist the corner of the quilted bedspread. "Like I said earlier, Eli's one of the nicest men I've ever met. He's strong and yet he's humble. I really admire that about him." She paused and added, "He reminds me of Daddy."

Chapter Nineteen

By 5:30 the next morning, Kate was up and ready to start anew. She'd had a dream about finding Paul that had stayed with her after she awoke. In her dream, he was grinning from ear to ear as she ran into his outstretched arms.

When she awoke, she felt certain that this would be the day they would find him. But when they reached Sugarlands to load up the vans, it was obvious that not everyone felt the same way. She glanced at the weary faces. Ranger Morton looked especially tired, and Kate thought his body language even suggested that he was ready to throw in the towel. He wouldn't make eye contact with her, and when she tried to talk to him, he excused himself and went to talk to one of the other rangers.

Kate was glad to see that Joe Tucker had rejoined the search since the doctors said that Sam was out of imminent danger.

"Why does everyone look so defeated?" she asked Sheriff Roberts.

He hesitated as if he didn't want to tell her, then said, "As many cold nights as we've had . . . it's more and more likely that we won't find them." He met her eyes. "I'm sorry, Kate."

"How can you say that?" Kate searched his face. "This is Paul, Sheriff. We can't give up the search."

"I feel the same way, and we're not giving up. Not yet. But I just want you to start preparing yourself for the worst." He placed a hand on her shoulder. The words struck her as if she'd been slapped.

"We found Paul's medicine bottle," she reminded him. "And he left us a trail to lead us to him. He and Marcus are out there. We have to find them. I'm sure we're not far now."

The sheriff nodded. "I know, I know," he said. "We haven't given up yet. Hopefully we'll find something today." Then he patted her arm and turned to the others who were drinking coffee. "Let's load 'em up!" he said to the Copper Mill searchers.

Even though they were continuing the search, Kate couldn't help but feel deserted. It seemed the team's leaders were giving up, at least in spirit.

She glanced around the room as searchers talked in quiet morning voices and sipped steaming coffee. She noticed a man who she figured must have just joined the search-and-rescue team. His back was to her, but she knew she hadn't seen him with the group before, because she surely would have noticed that black, gelled hair.

As if he could read her thoughts, he turned to

the side, offering her a better view. He was talking to a shorter man, also with black hair. Just then someone moved into her line of sight, and Kate stepped aside to look again.

When the shorter of the two men turned again, she saw his face—that flat nose and pale eyes. She knew him instantly. She moved through the crowd to get a closer look at his partner and immediately recognized that cleft in his chin. His dark eyes met hers.

She flinched, then glanced around and hurried to the back of the room where Sheriff Roberts was giving last-minute instructions to one of the volunteers.

"Sheriff Roberts," she whispered urgently. "They're here. Those strange men who came to my house. Come with me."

The sheriff's eyes widened as Kate reached for his hand and began to tug him over to where she'd seen the two men.

But when they got to the place where the men had been, they were gone. Kate frantically scanned the room, which was quickly emptying as searchers headed for the vehicles. Then she and the sheriff rushed outside, but there was no sign of them.

It was as if they'd vanished into thin air.

"They were here, Sheriff! I saw them!" Kate said.

The sheriff nodded, still looking around. "We'll keep an eye out."

It was now crystal clear to Kate. Those men had everything to do with Marcus' disappearance.

KATE SAT WITH REBECCA on the drive to the service road just north of Clingmans Dome Road. They bounced and jostled against each other on the faint track that was overgrown with spruce and fir trees. The woods were very dark and foreboding in that section of the park, not the light, colorful forest of the previous sections they'd searched.

Kate kept thinking about the two men, wondering where they had gone. Had they decided to follow the search party in hopes of beating them to Marcus? Or did they already have Paul and Marcus hidden someplace? But if they did, why would they try to infiltrate the search team? To taunt them? To find a way to . . . what? She wished she knew.

"This is ridiculous!" James Jenner's voice broke into her thoughts.

He was seated between his parents just behind Kate, in the back of the fifteen-passenger van. Justin rode shotgun at the front of the van, blissfully unaware of his family's argument. Kate glanced back to see Livvy shaking her head at her son.

"Keep your voice down," Kate heard Danny whisper.

She assumed he was hoping that nobody had heard them. She glanced back at him and saw that his face was red and he looked ready to burst. Embarrassed for him, she turned back around in her seat.

"Why do you keep bringing this up?" Kate heard Livvy whisper. "We already told you we're staying here until we bring Pastor Hanlon home."

"Fine!" James said in a low voice. "Then you can stay

here, but I have commitments at home that I have to get back to. At least let *me* go home alone. I need to be there to rehearse for Sunday's concert."

"There's not going to be any concert," Danny hissed. "That's what you can tell your friends."

Kate wanted to jump in and tell them that it was okay, that she and Paul would understand that James had obligations. Who could expect a teenager to drop everything to search for his pastor? But from the tone of Danny's voice, she knew better than to utter a word.

James began to argue, but his father cut in.

"Don't push me on this, James. We've already had this conversation."

"It's not as if your father and I aren't missing work to help look for Pastor Hanlon," Livvy added, "but some things are more important than work . . . Like friends!"

Kate felt as though Livvy was looking directly at her when she said the words, and tears of gratitude filled her eyes.

"The guys in the band are *my* friends, Mom. And you don't even know what the concert is all about. We just need to practice so I'm ready by Sunday. The guys have been texting me about it—"

"I'll take that phone, young man," Danny demanded. "These friends of yours are no friends. If they were, they'd understand that you have other obligations, and they'd stop trying to manipulate the situation."

"Give me my phone!" James' voice rose in volume.

At that, the rest of the van grew quiet, and heads

turned to see what all the fuss was about. James reached for the phone, which his father reluctantly returned to him.

"Turn it off," Danny said in a low voice.

Livvy's face had gone red. She met Kate's eyes and mouthed, "I'm sorry."

Kate shook her head and gave her friend a sympathetic look. She could understand both perspectives, and her heart went out to Livvy and Danny. Raising a teenage son was no easy task, especially in the midst of a crisis.

When the van finally stopped to let the group out, Kate could already hear search dogs barking up ahead. Each searcher piled out of the van and secured their backpacks. When Kate finally got out, she turned to Livvy who was behind her.

"Are you okay?" she asked her friend.

"I'm fine. I'm just sorry. You don't need this on top of everything else." She sighed. "It's like James is compelled. I don't understand it. Why can't he just accept things as they are and stop pushing?" She shook her head. "I'm so sorry, Kate."

"You don't need to be sorry," Kate assured her. "Friendship goes both ways. I've raised a son, so I totally understand."

Livvy's face broke into a smile. "Thank you."

Kate squeezed her hand.

Before long the group had spread out again as they had the past two days and resumed calling for Paul and Marcus, scanning for any sign of the men's trails or their presence, listening for the faintest sound but hearing only the barking of search dogs and the whir of helicopters.

Kate climbed over the trunk of a thick tree that had fallen in a storm, and Eli reached out a hand to help her. She nodded her thanks, glad she'd remembered to bring her hiking stick, then gazed ahead. It was a chilly morning, with temperatures in the midfifties, so she'd worn a fleece that she knew she'd eventually have to remove after she began generating heat from all the hiking. But she was glad she had it on right then as the cool air nipped at her cheeks.

As she came around a bend on a trail that rose at a gradual angle, Kate caught sight of a piece of cloth hanging from a tree branch up ahead.

She hurried toward it and shouted, "There's something here!" Eli and Rebecca were at her side almost immediately, as was Sheriff Roberts. The Jenners, Wilsons, and Joe were too far ahead to hear Kate's announcement.

Kate recognized the cloth the moment she saw it. It was a strip of fabric from one of Paul's Columbia shirts. She took the cloth in her hands to examine it more closely. It looked as if it had been torn deliberately into a four-inch strip, and there was blood on it. A chill ran down her spine at the implications. She looked around the clearing and saw another piece of material on the ground. She hurried over to the spot and bent down to pick up the cloth.

"Do you recognize it?" the sheriff asked.

"It's Paul's," she confirmed.

She turned to scan the area. Directly behind them,

and a couple dozen yards away, was a creek with a small cave along its banks. The cave's roof was only three feet from the ground, so there was no way anyone could stand inside it, but it might have provided shelter from the previous day's rain.

She pointed at it and said, "Let's look over there."

The sheriff pulled the radio from his belt and called to inform Ranger Morton.

When Kate reached the spot, with Eli, Rebecca, and the sheriff at her side, Kate could see that it was a campsite. Ashes from a burned-out fire made a circle in the dirt directly in front of the cave, and low-hanging branches looked as if they had been cut by a saw. Kate remembered that Paul had a small handsaw, though she couldn't recall if he'd packed it among his things.

Eli squatted down next to the fire and held out a hand to test its warmth. "It's stone cold," he said as he stood back up. He placed his hands on his hips.

"He built a fire," Kate said to herself, relieved that he'd been able to keep warm. "He wouldn't have used green wood for a fire," she said as she examined the cut tree branches.

"He could've used the branches for cooking food, though, if he was roasting fish or whatever," Eli suggested.

They looked around for any signs of a meal. There were several cattails laying on a rock.

"Are cattails edible?" Eli looked up at Sheriff Roberts.

"Yes, they are," the sheriff said. He scratched his chin and studied the fabric Kate had handed him.

"If he did catch some fish, he probably buried the remains in a different spot from where they were sleeping," Rebecca said. "To keep bears away."

Kate was glad Paul had taken their children on all those outdoor adventures and had taught them so much about wilderness survival. Of course, he'd never intended for them to ever have to use that knowledge.

Kate turned to survey the area. The air felt damp there, close, and a stream splashed down the rocky incline toward the valley below.

"Look at those rocks." Rebecca drew Kate's attention to a pile of moss-covered rocks at the stream's edge.

Kate joined her and bent to examine the jagged, slippery surface.

"That one looks like someone slipped on it," she said. "See how it's torn?"

The mossy surface was smeared, revealing the shiny, wet rock face beneath. It confirmed what Kate already suspected when she saw the torn fabric.

"Someone's hurt," she said when she stood back up. "Paul wouldn't tear up his brand-new shirt for any other reason."

By NOON THEY'D JOINED back up with Ranger Morton's team and had reached Clingmans Dome Road. The search dogs barked, urging the group up along the steep road along the Appalachian Trail. The road was closed during winter months because it was simply too treacherous to traverse with the complications of snow and ice.

Myriad questions passed through Kate's head as she walked along. Who was injured? And how badly? Did the strange men have anything to do with it? But that didn't seem to make sense, since she'd just seen the men that morning at the visitor center. How did they know about the search for Marcus? Had they seen it on the news, or had they followed Kate and Rebecca when they'd driven to Gatlinburg on Monday night?

She shook off the lingering questions and thought about the campsite they'd found. Did Paul have adequate clothing to stay warm without the thick wool shirt? She prayed he'd taken something else, a jacket or a fleece, perhaps. But she doubted it, since it hadn't been as cold when he'd first gone looking for Marcus.

Kate glanced at Joe, who had come up alongside her and was climbing the road with the rest of the group. He'd amazed Kate these past few days, not only with his knowledge of the area and his ability to handle the difficult terrain, but also with his sheer stamina for someone so old . . . not to mention his kindness.

Joe had reported that the doctors wanted to run some tests on Sam, so Sam was stuck in the hospital for the foreseeable future. But according to Joe, Sam wouldn't allow Joe to sit by his bedside for another minute when Paul was still missing. Kate was just glad Sam was okay. She wouldn't have been able to live with herself if the search for Paul had caused him harm—or worse.

Rebecca and Eli were up ahead. Her blonde head was tilted toward him, her ponytail swinging from the back of

her Tennessee Bucs baseball cap. Eli must have said
something funny because Rebecca had broken out in her
musical laugh. Kate watched them. They had an easy way
about them. Rebecca lit up whenever he was near, and
Eli's face would flame in that embarrassed yet pleased
expression Kate had seen many times in the past few days.

Kate so liked the young man that a part of her wished
it would work out between the two of them. Yet she knew
how conflicted Rebecca felt about the relationship, especially after pledging her love to Marcus. She was glad her
daughter was a person of honor, but if Marcus wasn't wor-
thy of her, then what?

Kate's ears popped, and the ache in her legs told her
she was climbing higher. She paused to rub her arthritic
knee and gazed at the now-familiar Clingmans Dome.
The awe-inspiring observation tower loomed ahead, with
its 375-foot ramp that wound to the top in a spiral. The
morning's fog had lifted for the most part, though patches
of it clung to sections of the valley below them. Several
members of the search team had walked past the tower
toward the Forney Ridge Trail where the dogs were sniffing around.

That was when Kate saw the strange men again. Even
though they were a good fifty yards ahead, she knew it was
them. They appeared to be searching like the rest of the
team, but Kate knew it was a front. But why, *why* would
they so openly show their faces in public when they knew
Kate and Rebecca were around? She was sure they were
involved in Marcus' disappearance, and the fact that they

were posing as searchers unnerved her. The sheer audacity of it made her mind spin.

"Rebecca," she called ahead, trying to regulate her voice so only Rebecca could hear and not the men she was drawing closer to.

Rebecca turned toward her, as did Eli.

"Look." Kate pointed to the closer of the two men. "It's them."

Rebecca looked, then nodded at her mother as her eyes widened. "It's them all right."

Kate and Joe caught up to where Eli and Rebecca were standing.

"So, what do we do?" Rebecca whispered.

Eli was already pulling off his pack and retrieving his walkie-talkie. Pressing the TALK button, he called for Sheriff Roberts.

"What do you have, Eli?" the sheriff's voice came over the air.

"Kate and Rebecca spotted the men who showed up at their home on Sunday. We need you over here ASAP."

"I'll bring company," he replied, then the walkie-talkie clicked off.

Kate looked ahead where the search-and-rescue team continued carefully scouring the woods west of the two men. With the sheriff on his way, she felt no need to alert the team about the men . . . at least not yet.

Within fifteen minutes, the sheriff and Ranger Morton arrived, along with two more officers. Kate pointed in the direction of the two men and was thankful that they seemed oblivious that they'd been spotted. Within seconds, the strangers were surrounded by officers. Kate, Joe, Rebecca, and Eli joined them.

"What are your names?" Sheriff Roberts boomed authoritatively.

"What's this all about?" one of the men said. The taller man's penetrating eyes shifted between the sheriff and Kate, who crossed her arms over her chest.

"We have reason to believe you are responsible for the disappearance of Marcus Kingsley, aka Mack Kieffer, and Paul Hanlon."

"Isn't that what this search is for, to find out where those two men are?" he asked. He lifted his shoulders in a shrug and looked at his partner.

"Listen," the stumpy man said, "we're volunteers here just like everyone else. We came to help!"

"Have you seen these women before?" Sheriff Roberts pointed to Kate and Rebecca, undeterred.

Both men looked at them, and Kate felt a fire spread over her cheeks.

"No, sir," the smaller one said in a thick East Coast accent. "We haven't seen them anywhere."

"Where did you say you were from?" Kate asked.

"We didn't." The taller guy turned to her. "Listen, lady, I don't know what you have to gain by accusin' your own search crew of . . . I don't even know what! But you're gonna drive away good help with an accusation like that. We're decent, honest guys who came out 'cuz we heard you were in need, but if you're gonna accuse us of doing somethin' to your husband, well . . ." He shook his head. "It just ain't right."

Kate turned to look at Rebecca. She was staring at the man in disbelief, watching his mouth as he spoke. She glanced up to see that the sheriff had gone into a huddle with the local authorities. Eli and Joe both stood watch with arms crossed over their chests like Roman sentries. Finally Sheriff Roberts pulled Kate aside.

"We don't have any evidence to arrest them, Kate," he said.

"It *is* them," she said.

"I'm sure you're right," the sheriff went on, "but knocking on your door and asking if you've seen someone isn't a crime. Unless we have some physical evidence that they've done something wrong, I can't take them into custody."

"What about the ring? They stole Rebecca's ring," she said, feeling desperate but trying to keep her tone controlled.

"Can you prove that?"

"They were at the house when it disappeared," Kate reminded him. "And the car they drove was stolen."

At that the sheriff radioed Sugarlands and asked them to have the police search the parking lot. Then he said to Kate, "I'll pat them down and check their gear, but that's all I can do for now."

He returned to the men and searched for any sign of the missing ring, but there was nothing in their pockets. The smaller of the two sneered at Kate. She looked away, wanting to scream in frustration.

Several moments later, the sheriff's radio buzzed.

"Sheriff Roberts here."

"Yes, sir. This is Officer Downey from the Gatlinburg police. We were in the neighborhood and were able to get to the Sugarlands lot quickly. We checked for that stolen vehicle you described and took the liberty of running all the plates that were there. There wasn't a stolen car among them."

Kate hung her head knowing what she wished she could prove: that these men were guilty of much. But of how much, she couldn't say.

Kate watched the men the rest of the afternoon, as they descended Forney Ridge Trail and stopped at Andrews Bald. They had acted offended at their unjust treatment, yet they hadn't stopped searching. It was the strangest thing.

The one comfort she took from it was that if the men were with them in the search, they weren't with Paul and Marcus doing who knew what. But then again, she also didn't know what kind of damage they had already done.

Kate lifted her gaze to the spectacular view, as one ridgeline met another in a hazy progression of rusty slopes, and her heart sent out an involuntary prayer to the Creator of this beauty. She reminded herself of God's faithfulness, and her heart found momentary solace in the thought.

Yet as the day continued to tick by, Kate knew that everyone was beyond exhausted. She felt the same. But

she couldn't give up on the search, on Paul, and she hoped
those in charge wouldn't either. Her heart throbbed with
pain whenever she thought about Paul. She'd loved that
man for almost thirty years. This wasn't how she'd envisioned the end of his life. It was too random, too trite
for Paul. He was a man of vision, a commanding leader.
For him to disappear in the woods . . . there was just something wrong about it. When it was his time to leave this
earth, she wanted him to be surrounded by loved ones, not
alone on a cold mountainside.

Kate shook off the morose thoughts. She didn't want
to face the fact that Paul could be dead. He was too smart
for that. In her heart she knew it. Paul could walk out of
these woods if he wanted to. Something was keeping him
from it.

Chapter Twenty

Kate finished getting ready for bed. Rebecca hadn't come back to the room yet, and Kate suspected she was talking with Eli. Was this their fourth night here? She could barely keep track. The days had melted together into one torturous eternity. Discouragement ate at her and left her feeling jittery. How she longed for sleep, and yet even in sleep, she was weary as one nightmare led to the next.

She'd just gotten off the phone with Marcus' sister, MaryAnne, who wasn't able to book a flight to Knoxville until the following day. There, she would rent a car and drive to Gatlinburg to join them. Kate had heard the worry in her voice.

"Everything that can be done is being done to find your brother," Kate had assured her. "Hopefully he'll be out of the woods by the time you get here, and you can simply help him recover."

MaryAnne thanked her, then hung up.

Then Kate called Melissa and Andrew to update them on the search for their father. Both offered consolation, but Kate could hear the worry in their voices as well. She stared at the phone after she hung up.

I want to call with news that Paul is safe, she thought. *No more calls like these.*

New questions had been nagging at Kate since they left the search that afternoon. Now that she knew that the strangers weren't with Paul and Marcus, what was keeping search and rescue from finding them? They'd certainly found enough signs that they were on the right track.

The pieces of Paul's shirt came to mind, and Kate sent up a prayer for whoever was injured. She hoped it wasn't anything serious, though it wouldn't take much, compounded with sleeping in the cold, to take a person to a life-threatening state.

A panicked knock sounded on Kate's door. She glanced at the clock. It was only ten, though it felt much later. Kate went to answer it and felt a moment of fear before opening the door, as she thought of the men they'd confronted on the trail. But what she found instead was a distraught-looking Livvy on the other side. She was wringing her hands.

"What's wrong?" Kate asked.

"Have you seen James?"

Kate could hear the worry in Livvy's voice as she scanned the room behind Kate.

"No. Is he missing?"

"We can't find him, and after our argument in the van this morning, I'm afraid of what he could've done. He was so angry all day . . ."

Kate's heart went out to her friend. She reached for Livvy's arm and pulled her into the room.

"Okay, take a deep breath," Kate said.

Livvy did as she was told, then her eyes searched Kate's.

"So, when did you see him last?" Kate asked.

Livvy exhaled before speaking. "Just after supper. He told us he was going to go play his guitar in the motel rec room."

The room that adjoined the manager's office consisted of several video-game stations, pool and Ping-Pong tables, as well as candy and soda vending machines.

"When we went to get him to tell him it was time to go to bed, he wasn't there, and he didn't answer his cell phone."

"Did you ask the manager if he'd seen him?"

Livvy nodded. "He told Danny that James was there for maybe half an hour. Said he was on his cell phone talking to someone, then he left."

"He could have simply gone for a walk and lost track of the time," Kate offered, but the expression on Livvy's face told her that Livvy's mother's intuition wasn't buying the explanation.

"Do you think he would've hitchhiked back to Copper Mill?" Livvy asked. "It would be a crazy thing to do, but I know he didn't have any money."

"First, let's ask around the motel. Maybe he's talking in someone's room," Kate said, hoping they'd find him chatting with one of their friends at the motel. "Let me get dressed." Kate retrieved her clothes from the dresser and went into the bathroom to change back into day wear.

"We should've listened to him," Livvy was saying when Kate came back out. "I'm afraid we pushed him too far, and now he's—" She blew out a breath and rubbed a hand across her forehead. "I remember what it was like to be a teenager, thinking I knew better than my parents. And Danny can get so stubborn if the boys don't listen to him."

"Most fathers are the same way," Kate assured her.

She led the way to the motel's outdoor corridor and Joe Tucker's room. After several long minutes, Joe answered their knock, looking as if he'd been asleep for quite some time.

"What's going on? Did someone find Paul?" he asked.

"No. I'm sorry to wake you, Joe," Kate said. "We're wondering if you might have seen James."

The wizened old man looked at Livvy, an eyebrow raising in worry. "That boy of yours took off?"

"I don't know," Livvy said, shaking her head.

"I saw him down by the pop machine," he said, confirming what the manager had already told Danny.

Kate said, "Why don't you head back to bed, Joe? You've had a long day already. We'll find him."

"Are you sure?" Joe said. "I'd be happy to get my duds back on and come look with you."

"No, that's okay," Livvy said. "We'll ask if any of the others have seen him."

But nobody else had seen James either. Sheriff Roberts headed out in his squad car to search the immediate area, while Kate and Livvy returned to the Jenners' room, where Justin was still sleeping. The fourteen-year-old had gone to bed early. He roused when they came into the room.

"What's going on?" he asked, lifting his head from the pillow and opening bleary eyes.

"Is Daddy here?" Livvy asked.

Justin rubbed his eyes and said, "I don't think so. Why?"

Livvy sat on the edge of the bed and touched his hair. "We can't find James. We think he might've tried to find a way to get back home, but—"

"Oh no!" Justin said, interrupting his mother. "I didn't think he'd actually do it!"

"Do what?" Livvy asked, glancing at Kate.

Justin looked as if he didn't want to tell his mother what his brother had confided to him. Finally he asked, "It's okay to break a promise if it's something really important, right?"

"You have to tell us what he told you," Livvy said. "He could be in danger, Justin. You need to tell us."

Justin thought about it for a moment, then said, "He said something about taking the Greyhound out of Knoxville and going back home. You don't think he'd actually do that, do you?"

"Knoxville?" Kate was stunned.

"Yesterday," Justin said, "when it was raining so hard and we were all stuck in the visitor center waiting to go look for Mr. Hanlon, he went online and looked up bus information. He said the nearest Greyhound station was in Knoxville."

"But Knoxville is over forty miles away. Did he mention how he planned to get there from here?" Kate asked.

Justin shook his head. Kate and Livvy exchanged a worried look as Danny came into the room, his expression frantic.

"Any word?" Danny asked.

"No," Kate said, "but Justin says he thinks James is on his way to Knoxville to take the Greyhound home."

"Where would he get the money for a bus ride?" Danny said, looking to his younger son.

Justin's gaze turned to the bedspread. "He . . . uh . . . he took it from Mom's purse."

Kate saw Livvy's face fall and placed an arm around her friend's shoulder. Danny was already on the phone, first to Sheriff Roberts and then to Information to find out the number for the Greyhound station in Knoxville.

"What did the sheriff say?" Livvy asked when he hung up.

"He's radioing ahead to Knoxville. The police and sheriff's departments will be on the lookout for him, and Sheriff Roberts is going to head toward the highway to see if he can spot him."

Just then a knock sounded on the door. Kate opened it to see Rebecca and Eli standing there, looking confused.

"I was wondering where you were," Rebecca said to her mother.

"I'm sorry," Kate said. "I should have left you a note."

Rebecca glanced at Livvy and said, "What's going on?"

She and Eli came into the room, and Kate filled them in about James.

"I'm so sorry," Rebecca said to Livvy. "This is awful."

Kate glanced at Justin, who looked as if he was about to cry. He was still in bed in his pajamas, sitting up and looking just like a little boy.

Danny had been talking on the phone with the Knoxville bus station. When he hung up the phone, he said, "There isn't a bus leaving for Chattanooga until seven o'clock in the morning," he said, "and so far they haven't seen anyone matching James' description."

"Did they say they'd call if he showed up?" Livvy asked.

"Yes," Danny said. "But until he gets there, who knows what kind of trouble he could get himself into. We need to go looking." He turned his eyes to Kate.

"We can take my car," she offered.

"I can stay with Justin if you guys would like," Rebecca offered.

"I'm not a baby!" Justin protested as he climbed out of bed.

"How about if we both stay with you?" Eli said, looking at Rebecca.

"Actually," Danny said, smiling at his fourteen-year-old, "that would be very helpful. It's been a long day already, and I know Justin needs his sleep."

"Dad!" Justin whined.

Danny shook his head. "The police are looking for James. We've covered all our bases. There's no reason that you need to come, Justin. Just stay here with Eli and Rebecca. We'll be back as soon as we can."

Kate, Livvy, and Danny piled into Kate's Honda. Kate

suggested that Danny drive, sensing he needed something to do to keep himself busy. It was past eleven o'clock, and the streets of Gatlinburg were quiet, except for the occasional car meandering past. Kate was in the backseat, her gaze glued to the left side of the road, while Livvy scanned the right side from the front seat.

"I wish I knew which route he took," Danny complained.

"How long ago did he leave the rec room?" Kate asked.

"The manager said he was there half an hour," Livvy reminded her, "so that means he left around eight o'clock."

"It's been three hours," Kate said. "Odds are he's already at the highway."

Danny pushed the accelerator and wove north toward State Highway 441.

As they reached the edge of town, Kate caught sight of someone walking in the opposite direction back toward Gatlinburg. The boy was tall and stocky, like James, with dark curly hair.

"That's him!" Kate said, pointing.

Livvy let out a sigh of relief, and Danny pulled the car alongside his son and shut off the engine. The three of them got out. James raised his head when they approached. The street light revealed a tear-stained face.

He shoved his hands into his pockets as Livvy pulled him into a deep embrace.

"I was so worried," she said.

"I'm sorry, Mom," James replied.

"What were you thinking?" Danny asked, tension etched in his face. "Something could have happened to

you! We were all worried sick. Even the police are out looking for you." His voice rose in pitch with each sentence.

James lowered his head and said, "It was stupid, and
I'm really sorry." He shrugged, looking forlorn.

"Why were you walking back toward town?" Livvy asked.

"I realized I was being selfish and decided to come
back," he said.

Danny pulled his cell phone from his pocket and
flipped it open.

"Sheriff, this is Danny Jenner," he said. "We found
him." He paused as the sheriff said something, then continued. "Thank you for everything. I can't tell you how
much we appreciate it." He said good-bye and closed the
phone.

James reached into his pocket, pulled out the cash
he'd taken from his mother, and handed it to her. Tears
streamed down Livvy's cheeks, and Kate placed a comforting hand on her friend's back.

"I'm so disappointed that you did that," Livvy said to
her son. "To steal money—"

"I know," he said quietly.

"Let's go back to the motel," Danny said.

They climbed back in Kate's car. This time Livvy took
the backseat with her son, while Kate sat up front with
Danny.

"You need to know that there will be consequences for
this," Danny said after several minutes of driving. He
looked into the rearview mirror so he could make eye contact with James.

Kate glanced back.

James had turned his gaze to the floor, and Livvy was holding his hand.

When they reached the motel, Danny seemed to have cooled off quite a bit, though Kate sensed there would be a family discussion about what had happened. He'd already mentioned pulling James out of the band, and the boy had only nodded, as if he knew he was getting what he deserved.

Danny handed the car keys to Kate and escorted his son back to their room, while Livvy stayed behind. Her tear-filled gaze met Kate's.

"I'm sorry about tonight," she said.

"You've apologized too many times already," Kate said, hugging Livvy.

When Livvy pulled back, she said, "I got a glimpse tonight of what you must be feeling this week with Paul missing—" Her voice cracked, and she wiped the tears from her cheeks. "I thought I understood before, but it's not the same."

"Livvy," Kate said, "it's okay."

"It's *not* okay," Livvy said. "It won't be okay until we bring Paul home."

By Friday, half of the search-and-rescue team had moved on to other calls. Kate couldn't blame them. After all, people had obligations. But with fewer searching, it meant that the likelihood of finding Paul and Marcus alive was also reduced by that much.

Kate hadn't seen the two men they'd confronted the previous day. And that concerned her more than comforted her because it meant that she couldn't keep an eye on them. She scanned the conference room where Ranger Morton was briefing the remaining search crew on that day's search plan. Even the number of reporters had dwindled to a lone man with a notepad.

The plan was to split into two groups, one for each of the trails that led into the backcountry from Andrews Bald just south of Clingmans Dome.

Kate stretched her aching back and neck muscles. She wasn't looking forward to another day of hiking, and after the events of the previous night, she hadn't gotten much sleep.

Finally they loaded into vehicles and drove to the trailhead to begin another day of searching. It had become a routine of sorts. All of the searchers knew their roles. Dogs sniffed along the ground, and helicopters scanned the terrain from above, while the search-and-rescue workers called out the missing men's names with no response.

Occasionally a view would open up along the trail, a gorgeous panorama of color, with mists adding a gossamer effect to the portraits beyond. Danny Jenner and his boys moved out to the east of Kate, while Livvy walked by her side.

"Hey, you," Livvy said.

Kate glanced at her dear friend.

"How are you holding up?"

Kate shrugged. "I've been better."

She reached for Kate's hand and gave it a squeeze before letting it go.

They walked for three hours without any sign of Paul or Marcus, not a campsite or granola wrapper or strip of fabric to be seen. Kate kept calling Paul's name, but even that had become rote. She didn't expect an answer.

Something just didn't seem right. Kate could sense it in her core. They'd come up that long stretch of road to get where they were now. If Paul and Marcus had come all the way to Clingmans Dome Road, why hadn't they just waited for help? There were plenty of cars that traversed the road to the lookout tower, especially in the glorious days of autumn. Someone would have found them and taken them to safety.

She pictured the dogs the previous day at Andrews Bald moving from one path to the next. She glanced at Livvy as a thought came to her, then lifted her face to the cool September day.

"We've lost the trail," she said quietly.

"What did you say?" Livvy turned to her.

"Marcus and Paul didn't come to the highest point," Kate said. "It doesn't make sense. They're still walking in circles to the north."

"What do you mean?" Livvy asked.

"Once Paul reached the road, he wouldn't have gone back into the wilderness. The dogs are leading us on a wild goose chase."

Livvy gave that some thought. "But we would've seen him on the road."

"That's why I think he never made it to the road."

"Kate, I can't even think straight anymore," Livvy confessed. "None of this makes sense. We're guessing at everything here!"

"No, we aren't," Kate corrected. "We found his prescription bottle and those strips of fabric. And those weren't left by a bear."

Livvy laughed.

"And we know where they camped just south of Chimney Tops. We've just lost their trail. Someone was injured. We know that much from the pieces of Paul's shirt and the marks on the rocks. That would've slowed them down, not bolstered them to climb all the way up here. What if we walked right past them and didn't see them because they can't respond?"

Kate stopped walking and looked her friend in the eyes. "First we were trying to think like Marcus. But I think that's leading us nowhere. We need to try to think like Paul," Kate said, feeling frustrated by the lack of clarity in her thoughts until that moment.

"Without knowing what circumstances he's in, that's awfully hard to do," Livvy observed.

"I've been married to him almost thirty years. I know him better than anybody."

Kate gazed into the woods. Morning light filtered through the balding treetops. The ground was a carpet of yellow and red.

"I know I'm right," she said. "Paul would never have come this way, not if he passed the road."

She called to Sheriff Roberts, who was part of her search team and told him her conclusions.

"But the dogs picked up a scent," he protested.

"And dogs are never wrong?" Kate asked. "Think about it, Sheriff. If Paul stumbled onto the road, he wouldn't have kept going. He'd be hitchhiking for help!"

The rotund man rubbed his chin in thought. "What do you propose we do?" he finally asked.

"I propose that we don't waste another precious minute." Kate replied. "We've already lost three hours today."

IT WAS JUST PAST NOON by the time the search-and-rescue team made it back up Forney Ridge Trail. Ranger Morton and the local crew were standing in a circle in private conversation when Kate and the others arrived. When she joined them, the words she heard coming from one of the crew members she hadn't been introduced to sent a wave of shock through her system.

"This search has already cost us thousands of dollars—" the man was saying.

"Mrs. Hanlon," Ranger Morton cleared his throat in an obvious attempt to get the man to stop talking.

"We've lost the trail," Kate agreed with the man. "We need to go back to the campsite from yesterday and pick it up from there."

"We've scoured that whole area," the man said.

"What if we walked right by them?" Kate kept her cool, though it wasn't easy. Rebecca came up beside her and placed a hand on her back. "What if they're injured and can't respond?"

"It's Friday," Ranger Morton said. "Our odds are getting slimmer and slimmer."

"I don't care about odds," Kate said. "We can't give up!"

"I'm sorry, Mrs. Hanlon"—his voice was apologetic—"You expect us to change plans based on a hunch?"

Kate shrugged. "I know I'm asking a lot. But it's my husband."

"I'm sorry," he said. He lifted his face to those in the circle. "The crew is right." He made eye contact with the man who had been speaking when Kate first arrived. "This investigation has already cost too much, and the trail is cold. We need to go back to the drawing board."

"What are you saying?" Kate asked.

"I'm saying you're probably right about them not being down here, but that doesn't mean you're right about going back to where we've already searched. We need to figure out what we're doing or call off the search."

The ranger ordered everyone back in the vans to return to Sugarlands. As they drove east along the road, Kate's heart began to sink. How could she go home without Paul? She couldn't even fathom the thought. She glanced toward the van in front of theirs where Ranger Morton rode. She didn't want to feel angry at the man, and yet she was. Couldn't he understand how unthinkable it was to simply stop looking? Both vans slowed for another sharp turn around a curve. The views were breathtaking.

She peered through the woods to the north, hoping to

get a glimpse of Paul. Why couldn't she figure out where he was? Why couldn't she feel it in her bones? She was as connected to him as any person could be, and yet she still had no sense of where he was.

All along the road, she scanned for any sign of him and Marcus. But there was no sign.

She even looked along Newfound Gap Road, though she knew it would be impossible to walk that far in a few short hours.

The sheriff glanced back at her. He must have felt sorry for her because he radioed ahead to see if anyone had picked up the men. No one had. Paul and Marcus weren't anywhere to be found.

Chapter Twenty-One

Marcus was dying. Paul could see it in the glaze that covered the young man's eyes as fever swept his thin body. Paul checked the bandage that covered Marcus' broken arm. Blood stains had turned brown on the flannel sling that encased it, so he knew that the bleeding had stopped. Paul had managed to splint it with a green branch from a tree, but Marcus would need a doctor to assure that the arm would heal correctly.

Paul gently tugged the silver emergency blanket up across Marcus' body. The young man's head rested on Paul's backpack. Lying there, he looked more like a boy than a man. He took a shallow breath, then his eyes rolled and his eyelids closed.

They'd managed to find one of the three-sided lean-tos with wire mesh along the fourth wall. The structures dotted the Smoky Mountain backcountry, and had provided a measure of protection from the wind during the night, but it had done little to keep the cold, and the worry, at bay. Paul stood alongside the built-in bunk and watched him sleep.

What worried Paul most was that Marcus might already be beyond helping. No doubt he was dehydrated, though Paul had done everything he could to find water to drink. And the young man had lost weight. That was evident in the loose fit of his clothes.

Paul glanced at his own midsection, which had become considerably smaller in the past four days. Combined with the cold and the endless shivering that went with it, Paul wondered how they'd managed to survive this long. With Marcus' broken arm and now the fever, Paul felt certain an infection had set in. It signaled the end for the young actor, and Paul simply couldn't allow that. If he couldn't get Marcus out of these woods, the least he could do was bring help to Marcus.

He tugged his backpack up onto his bony shoulders and turned one last time to Marcus.

"I'm going for help, Marcus." To his own ears his voice sounded raspy and weak. "You stay here, okay? Try to keep warm in that bunk. I'll send help as soon as I can."

The young man didn't move, didn't lift his head to acknowledge that he'd heard what Paul said.

Paul turned and carefully shut the door, then set off toward the south. He'd been watching the sun's movement all morning, so he felt certain that he was going in the right direction, yet his body was exhausted to the point of collapse. He wished he still had his thick Columbia shirt. He felt so cold. Yet he willed himself forward, one step in front of the next, climbing over deadfall and pushing brush aside. He'd brought along several granola-bar wrappers he'd kept to mark his trail. These he tied to pine branches as he moved toward the ridge.

He'd been walking for a good hour, but the road he'd thought was just over the next hill was nowhere to be found. Thoughts of Marcus tugged at him. What if he was wrong? What if he couldn't find help for the young man? Would he die there all alone without even a friend at his side?

Paul stopped in his tracks and turned full circle. The sun was directly overhead. He lifted his face to it, wishing for the wisdom to know what to do.

Lord, he prayed, *don't let Marcus die back there. Keep him going.*

Then he turned back. At least at the lean-to there was a chance other hikers would come upon them. He prayed that Marcus would still be breathing when he got back.

As he neared the lean-to a good hour later, the sound of voices drew his attention. Paul quickened his step and called in his weakened voice, "Hello!" Someone had found them!

But when he was within fifty yards of the lean-to, he stopped in his tracks. Two dark-haired men wearing orange vests came out of the structure. They were carrying Marcus between them, one holding him under the arms and the other grabbing his legs. They looked like rescue workers, but the words coming out of their mouths stunned Paul.

"We got here too late. He's practically dead already!" the taller one said.

"We shoulda just killed him back in Jersey," the smaller one said. "Instead of chasin' him all over the country. That sheriff is onto us."

Panic tightened Paul's throat. These were the two men he'd seen at the Bristol the night before they'd left on the trip. What were they doing here in the middle of the wilderness? His answer came quickly when he saw one of them lay an unconscious Marcus on the ground and search his body. The smaller one patted him down and reached into his pockets. But when he began to tear at the bandages that covered Marcus' broken arm, Paul had seen enough.

He shouted at them as he charged over, "What do you think you're doing? Get away from him. Can't you see he's dying?"

The men raised their heads, obviously surprised at his presence. The taller one stood to his full height, a good six inches taller than Paul. He had a sneer on his face. Paul noted the other's peculiar stance, the way his knees pointed out while his toes pointed in.

"You must be that preacher they're all lookin' for," he said.

Hope flashed into Paul's consciousness right before the man landed a hard blow to Paul's midsection, knocking the wind from his lungs. Paul staggered back, gasping for air.

"They won't be findin' you anytime soon," the man snickered, taking another step toward Paul. He aimed for Paul's face, catching his right eye, which burned from the impact. Paul raised his fists and threw a right jab at the man's chin, but the man barely flinched.

"Is that all you got?" he laughed at Paul. Then he punched him hard again in the belly.

Pain radiated up Paul's torso, and he struggled to stay on his feet.

"Last I heard, that search team had totally lost your trail," the man said. "They're all down by Clingmans Dome! They'll never find you. And that pretty wife of yours—" He shook his head.

With those words, Paul mustered every ounce of his strength and clocked the man hard in the nose. Blood gushed from his nostrils, and he clutched his hands to his face, obviously stunned.

"My nose is bleedin'!" he raged, his eyes bulging. Blood dripped from between his fingers.

Paul moved forward for another blow, but the smaller of the two came in from behind.

"Oh no you don't!" the smaller man said. He kicked Paul's feet out from under him, and Paul crashed back, hitting his head against the hard ground.

Paul saw the trees overhead and heard the chirping of birds, and then everything faded to black. When he awoke, he had no idea how much time had passed. The sun was still bright in its westward arc, but the men and Marcus were gone. The contents of Paul's backpack lay scattered across the leaf-covered ground. He sat up and touched the place where his head had hit. He could feel dried blood on the spot. Taking a deep breath, he realized what had happened.

Marcus had been kidnapped.

Didn't those men understand that he was dying? What did they think they were going to do with him?

Paul stood to his feet, and the ground spun around him. He closed his eyes until the vertigo passed, then staggered to the lean-to. It was empty. Then, barely able to keep his balance, he walked. His body throbbed from the beating he'd taken, and his hand hurt from landing the punch on the tall man's nose. But it didn't matter. He'd failed Marcus, failed him miserably. He had to do everything within his power to help the young man.

He was no more than a hundred yards from the lean-to when he collapsed on a stone ledge, unable to walk, unable to do anything except lie there and consider his fate. He'd known that Marcus was dying. Now he knew that he too was at his journey's end.

Chapter Twenty-Two

"Are you saying you're quitting?" Kate heard herself shouting at the authorities around the large conference table at Sugarlands Visitor Center, but she felt like she couldn't help it. They were giving up on Paul. She couldn't comprehend it.

"I said I'm not saying that." Ranger Morton held up a hand like a policeman at an intersection. "We simply need time to reevaluate our search strategy. The helicopters have been all over this section of the park, and there's been nothing new to indicate where they are. If they'd gone east they would've hit Newfound Gap Road; south, and they would've come on the Appalachian Trail or Clingmans Dome Road. For all we know, they're walking in circles."

Kate rubbed her temples. A headache was coming on.

"Can we at least go look in the area where we found the campsite?" Eli said from the far side of the table. "Couldn't Mrs. Hanlon be right? Couldn't we have lost the trail there?"

"It's possible, but it's not probable. We've scoured that area already." The ranger sighed and said to Kate in a kind voice, "They've had little food or water since Monday night, and it's Friday. If they're moving at all . . ." He paused before adding, "Like I said, we're not quitting. We're just reevaluating."

"Reevaluating what?" Rebecca's voice rose in aggravation. Her cheeks were red, and her eyes sparked with indignation. "Whether or not Marcus' and Dad's lives are worth the cost to the State of Tennessee?"

Kate placed a hand on her daughter's knee in an attempt to calm her down. Then she glanced at Livvy, who gave her a sympathetic look.

"That's enough of that!" Sheriff Roberts snapped.

"Just let us look," Kate said to him, pleading. "Please, Sheriff Roberts. That's all we want to do."

"You can't go without guides. You'll get lost just like your husband and your daughter's friend," Ranger Morton said. "You're wasting your time."

The sheriff shot him a glare that silenced him.

"I can guide them," Joe Tucker spoke up. "I know these woods as well as any of your hired mugs!"

Sheriff Roberts considered the old man for what felt like many long moments.

"Okay," he finally said to Joe. "I'll go along if you guide us."

The ranger sputtered and the sheriff held up a forefinger.

"We'll be back by dark," he said simply.

It was three-thirty in the afternoon by the time they

reached the place where they would begin their hike to the cave where Paul had camped. Only the group from Copper Mill had come along for the search. The official search-and-rescue team had stayed at the visitor center.

Kate prayed fervently for some irrefutable sign that Paul had been there that morning, something that would force Ranger Morton and his men to resume the search.

The afternoon sun was warm on Kate's back as she positioned her walking stick to lower herself down the steep embankment to the more level area below. It was slow going. Eli helped her and Rebecca, supporting them with strong hands when they needed it. Danny and Livvy followed with their two boys and the Wilson brothers.

Rebecca moved up ahead with Joe, calling loudly for Paul and Marcus. Kate turned to glance at Eli, whose gaze followed Rebecca. His eyes crinkled into a smile. She could hear the others to her left, calling along their arc into the valley.

There were fallen logs scattered here and there on the ground, but for the most part, the walking wasn't too difficult once they'd gotten down the initial section. Deer trails wove among the rhododendron, blueberries, and sand myrtle. Birds took to flight, complaining at their presence.

Kate thought of Ranger Morton's warning that they were wasting their time. She prayed this wouldn't be another false start like their visit to the old man at the ramshackle cabin or their search below Clingmans Dome. So much depended on the outcome here. She knew if they didn't return with news of Paul or Marcus, they'd be returning to Copper Mill empty-handed. Not to mention brokenhearted.

Doubt pulled at Kate. It had been cold every night, with temperatures dipping down into the midforties. At the higher altitudes, it had been even colder. The men could have easily succumbed to hypothermia. Hadn't Ranger Morton said that hypothermia was one of the leading causes of death among lost hikers? She sighed heavily and shouted Paul's name again as she scanned for any variation in the landscape that might indicate his presence.

They'd been hiking for well over two hours when Kate saw what looked like a shack. She pointed to it, then she and Eli hurried over to see if it contained any sign of Paul or Marcus. Her heart beat in her chest at the thought that the men could be there.

When she drew closer, she could see that it was a three-sided lean-to, with wire mesh on the fourth side. Rebecca and Joe had seen it too; they were coming toward it from the east.

Kate came around to the other side, and there, lying on the ground, was Paul's backpack. It was opened, its contents strewn like debris.

When Sheriff Roberts radioed in with the news, all the ranger seemed able to say was, "Well, I'll be." Then he added, "We'll get the search-and-rescue team down there ASAP!"

Kate smiled gratefully at the sheriff. "I can't tell you . . . ," Kate began, but he held up a hand.

"Save that for when we bring Paul and Marcus home. You were right, Kate. You know your husband."

Then the radio crackled again. Sheriff Roberts lifted it to his mouth. "Roberts here."

Livvy came alongside Kate and placed an arm around her shoulders. Kate smiled at her friend as hope welled inside of her.

"Sheriff," Ranger Morton's voice came across the airwaves. "We just got a call from your deputy back in Copper Mill. A Skip Spencer?"

"What did he have to say?" The sheriff exchanged a puzzled look with Kate.

"He said he's been talking to people in town about those two men."

"Okay . . ." The sheriff tapped his finger on the side of the radio as if he couldn't end the conversation soon enough.

"Someone named Loretta Sweet said she talked to the men last Monday." He paused. "Your deputy said she told the men that Rebecca's new boyfriend—I'm assuming that's Marcus Kingsley—went camping with the church group."

Kate's eyes shot to Rebecca. A hand went to the young woman's mouth.

"We told her when we came in for lunch at the diner," Rebecca whispered more to herself than to anyone else. "We led them right to Marcus."

"And there's more," the ranger said. "He said they found that stolen El Dorado near Willy's Bait and Tackle. He said one of his mother-in-law's cars was stolen in its place, though he didn't notice it until this morning."

"So the theft hadn't been reported yet when we had the men for questioning yesterday?" the sheriff said.

Kate could hear the strain in his voice.

"Appears so, Sheriff."

Ranger Morton signed off, and Kate bent over to look at her husband's backpack. It had been slashed apart with a large knife.

"The two were here," Kate whispered.

THE SUN DIPPED LOW in the sky, warning that dusk was close at hand, but Ranger Morton still hadn't arrived with reinforcements. They waited at the lean-to, hoping Marcus and Paul would return. But no such luck. It had only been thirty minutes since they'd radioed with news of the find, but it felt like an eternity.

When Sheriff Roberts had inspected the ground around the lean-to more closely, it was apparent that a struggle had taken place. The lean-to's mesh was dented in several spots, though that could have happened over the natural course of its life. But the recent scuff marks in the dirt and the shredded backpack left no doubt that something awful had happened here.

Under the built-in bunk, he'd found the sci-fi-looking silver survival blanket on the floor. Kate confirmed that Paul had packed one. She picked up the pack and gathered Paul's things. She touched them lightly, gazing at each object as if through them she could sense where her husband was.

She wished she knew what had happened. Had Marcus attacked Paul? She hadn't considered that possibility before, and Rebecca had never mentioned Marcus having a violent temper. From what she'd seen of him, he seemed like a gentle man, though a bit jumpy. He didn't strike her as someone who would purposely hurt another person.

She bent down and reached for Paul's vitamin pillbox. He'd only planned on being there for three days, but she knew Paul. If he'd been stocking the seven-day container, he would have gone ahead and filled the whole week's worth.

Sure enough, only the supply for Saturday and Sunday remained. He would have taken his vitamins at home before he left on Sunday. She held the plastic container up for Sheriff Roberts to see.

"He was alive this morning," she said. "He faithfully took his vitamins."

Once she had finished looking at each object, she neatly put everything back, just as she knew Paul had packed it. Then she stood, ready to look around some more, though the group had already done a thorough sweep of the immediate area. There were more scuff marks to the west, and Sheriff Roberts noted two sets of footprints. Kate wanted to follow them, but the sheriff advised against it.

"It's just not safe, Kate," he said. "It's obvious that there was foul play. To send our group into danger . . ." He shook his head. "As an officer of the law, I just can't allow that. We're going to need to head back," he said, "or we'll be here all night."

"I don't care if I'm here all night," Kate said. "I'll sleep in the lean-to if I have to."

"We didn't bring supplies for an overnight stay," he reminded her.

Kate gazed toward the ridge that towered above. It was barely visible through the trees to the south.

"Let's go that way," she said, pointing at the mountaintop.

The sheriff nodded and spread the word that they were heading back to the road.

The group moved out, this time in single file, with Joe leading the way. They had gone about twenty yards when he stopped and pointed to the low branch of a pine tree.

"Take a look!" He grinned at Kate.

There, tied to the pine tree's thin branch was a granola-bar wrapper, its silver and green shimmered in the late-day sunshine. Kate turned her head to scan for another, and there it was, thirty yards away on a branch closer to the ridge.

"All right," the sheriff said to everyone, "Let's spread out again. Looks like we found his trail."

Kate stuck close to Livvy and Danny, looking for signs —broken twigs, disturbed foliage, or fallen leaves that had been stepped through. The breeze rustled the trees over-head. Kate shivered and lifted her gaze to the rocks that angled skyward. They rose to the embankment above in a sharp incline. It would be difficult climbing.

Then up ahead she saw something on a low rock ledge. She moved closer to get a better look, and at the same time, she heard the rustle of leaves. Fear shot through her. Was it a bear, or had those men laid a trap for them?

Chapter Twenty-Three

Within mere seconds of sighting the shape on the ledge, Kate's fear was overcome by joy. It wasn't a bear or the two men; it was Paul.

He lay on his back on the rock ledge. Joe must have seen him at the same time because he started yelling with Kate to the rest of the team.

"We found him! We found Paul!"

They ran to him. His eyes were closed, and his skin was pale and filthy. Kate noticed how thin he was, and she had an overwhelming urge to kiss his sunken cheek. When she leaned over him, she saw that he had bruises across his face and a cut above his eye. Tears streamed down her face as she stroked his cold forehead. His eyelids fluttered open. He looked confused and dazed, but he smiled when he saw her.

"They took him" was all he managed to get out before his eyes closed again.

The sheriff came to her side and bent down to look at Paul.

"He's been beaten," he said, lightly touching the cut on Paul's head. He gently lifted him and saw that the back of his head had a gash. It was caked with blood, and his right eye was swollen and black.

He looked horrible and yet he'd never looked better. Joy flooded Kate's being. She'd found him, and he was alive! She could scarcely believe it.

Paul's eyes fluttered, and he managed through chattering teeth, "They took Marcus. Some men. The two we saw that night at the restaurant . . ."

Kate could hear the panic in his exhausted voice.

"I tried to fight them, but there were two . . ." He took a shallow breath. "Marcus is dying, but they took him anyway."

"*Shh,*" Kate comforted, not wanting him to overexert himself. Yet his words disturbed her.

"Do you know which way they went?" Sheriff Roberts coaxed.

Paul's eyes drifted shut again, and this time they didn't open. Kate reached into her backpack for a bottle of water, but he was already unconscious.

She stroked his stubbled cheeks as a new fear arose. Had they gotten to him too late? Sheriff Roberts radioed in with the good news that they'd found Paul and the bad news that he had been beaten and was unconscious.

"We need medics here immediately," he announced to the Sugarlands manager, then gave the group's exact coordinates. Thankfully there was a big enough clearing nearby where a helicopter could land, since there were no roads close enough to safely carry Paul out on a stretcher.

The sheriff pocketed his radio and turned toward
Kate. "I'm beginning to think no one should be allowed in
these woods, this being the second call for medical help
since we got here."

Kate felt herself nodding in agreement. It *was* dangerous out here; not even safe for an Eagle Scout.

THE GROUP STOOD THERE, each person's patience clearly
waning as they waited for the medevac helicopter to
arrive. Kate glanced over at Rebecca, who was near her
father's feet. She had seen the fear in her daughter's eyes
when Paul confirmed that the men had taken Marcus.
What did they plan to do with him? That was a question
Kate didn't want to consider.

"What's this?" Eli said, drawing Kate from her thoughts.

The young man bent to the ground where Paul lay.
Tucked just underneath Paul's unconscious form was a
white slip of paper folded in half. He picked it up and
opened it. Then his face twisted in confusion for a
moment before he handed the paper to Kate.

"Isn't that your address?" he said.

The paper contained Paul and Kate's address in
Copper Mill, though it didn't mention their names. Kate
didn't recognize the handwriting; she knew it wasn't
Paul's. Livvy stood beside her, reading along. Kate turned
the paper over. The other side was blank.

"What is it?" Rebecca asked. Kate handed the sheet to
her daughter. Rebecca studied it for a moment, then
turned it over. "Just your address? What do you think it
means?"

"I don't know," Kate said. "I suppose those men proba-bly wrote it down to find Marcus. Though how they got our address in the first place is a mystery to me."

She showed the paper to Sheriff Roberts, then at his discreet nod, she put it back in her pocket. She knew that if she were anyone else, the sheriff wouldn't allow her to keep a piece of evidence, so she was thankful for his trust in her detective instincts.

Kate stuck close to Paul's side, holding his hand and stroking his arm. He remained unconscious, whether from hypothermic shock or mere lack of sleep, Kate couldn't tell. But it worried her.

When the helicopter finally arrived it was almost com-pletely dark outside. Dusk clung to the trees, with a mere shimmer of orange sunlight across their tops. The heli-copter landed, and an EMT crew hurried out to care for Paul. They checked his vital signs and loaded him onto the chopper. Before the pilot got back into the helicopter, he shouted above the roar of the blades, "I'll come back for all of you once we get him up to the hospital."

"Wait! I am coming with!" Kate shouted to the pilot.

"No, ma'am. I'm sorry, but we can only carry so many people on the chopper, and we're at capacity," he yelled.

Kate felt devastated that she couldn't go with her hus-band, but as she looked over at Rebecca, she realized that she needed to stay with her daughter and be a comfort to her. She put her arms around Rebecca as the helicopter lifted into the air, then she closed her eyes and prayed that this wouldn't be the last time she would see her husband alive.

LATER THAT NIGHT, after the helicopter had transported the group back to Sugarlands and they had talked with reporters, Kate and Rebecca drove to the Fort Sanders Sevier Medical Center in nearby Sevierville.

They stood at the foot of Paul's hospital bed while doctors and nurses checked vitals and spoke in hushed tones.

One of the doctors said that Paul wasn't "out of the woods." Kate found the statement ironic.

The EMTs had hooked him up to an IV en route and a heart monitor now beeped its faint rhythm on the far side of the bed. Warmed blankets covered his body since his core temperature had been far too low. He was badly dehydrated—the main reason for his continued comatose state, according to the doctor. They needed to pump his body full of fluids before his internal organs began to shut down.

As for the wounds he'd suffered in his fight with the men, he had a concussion from being knocked to the ground, but no broken bones.

Kate held his hand. She couldn't seem to take her eyes off him. She wanted to drink him in, make sure he was real. Finally the medical personnel left the room so they could be alone with Paul for their fifteen minutes of visiting time in the intensive care unit.

Rebecca moved to the edge of the bed and gently patted the blanket that covered his feet. Kate could see the unshed tears that shimmered in her eyes.

"I'm so worried, Mom," Rebecca said. "Daddy can't die now."

"He's going to be okay," Kate said, praying that God would honor her faith. She gazed at Paul's handsome face, the face she'd come to adore. Nearly thirty years of marriage had only solidified her love for him. It was no longer the flimsy, frail love of youth but was as firm and foundational as any rock. What would she do without Paul and his love? She didn't want to think about that. Instead, she reached for her daughter's hand, and together they prayed for Paul.

When their visiting time was over, they walked slowly down the hospital corridor. The sound of their boots on tile echoed in the lonely expanse.

Sheriff Roberts and the others were holding vigil in the ICU waiting room.

"How is he?" Livvy asked when Kate and Rebecca entered the room. Danny was next to her.

"Resting," Kate said, "but still unconscious."

"He's dehydrated," Rebecca took over. "We should know more by morning, once they can test him to make sure he doesn't have any organ damage."

A sobering hush fell across the room, and Kate noticed for the first time a short, heavyset blonde woman whom she hadn't seen before. The woman walked across the room and held out a hand to Kate.

"MaryAnne Kieffer," the woman introduced herself. At first Kate was confused, but then she realized this was Marcus' sister, who was scheduled to arrive that day. "I heard your husband was found and thought I'd come meet you here in case there was any news on Marcus...."

"Oh, MaryAnne, I'm so happy to see you. I'm sorry we don't have Marcus." The woman's face fell, then her eyes crinkled into a forced smile. She turned to Rebecca. "You must be the girlfriend. Marcus always did know how to get the pretty girls."

Rebecca blushed at the compliment and shook hands with her. Kate noticed Rebecca's glance shift to Eli, then back to the newcomer.

Then MaryAnne nodded at the sheriff before speaking, "The sheriff here tells me you found your husband around six or six-thirty . . ."

Kate nodded.

"And that two men beat him up and took Marcus." She shook her head. "Do you have any idea who they are or what they could want with him? I don't get it. We're hundreds of miles from New York. Who in the world would follow him and then kidnap him in the middle of the wilderness?"

"We were kind of hoping you could help us with that," Kate admitted.

Sheriff Roberts pulled a piece of paper from the inside pocket of his jacket and flattened it on a table, then handed it to the woman. "This is a composite drawing of the suspects."

It was nearly an exact likeness of the two men, down to the cleft in the taller man's chin and the flat nose and pale, sinister eyes of the smaller man.

MaryAnne gasped and clutched a hand to her mouth. "It's the Sacco brothers," she breathed as she lifted terrified eyes to Kate. "Jerry and Alex Sacco. They live in West Orange, or at least they used to when we were kids."

"Are you sure it's them?" Kate asked, remembering that 'Sacco' was the name Marcus had called the old squatter.

"I wish I weren't." She turned to the sheriff, fear in her eyes. "Those two boys . . . Well, let's just say that the last I heard, those two were in the banking business, so to speak."

"Meaning what?" Rebecca asked.

"They're . . . loan sharks," MaryAnne clarified.

"Loan sharks?" Rebecca's voice rose at least two octaves. "What would Marcus have taken out a loan for?"

"The kind of loans they give . . ."—MaryAnne paused and glanced around the room before going on—"They're usually for one of two things: drugs or gambling. And Mack, I mean Marcus, wouldn't think of touching any drugs. He's too smart for that, and besides, they'd wreck his good looks."

Kate glanced at her daughter and noticed that a dark cloud had formed across her brow.

"I hope they aren't the ones who took Marcus," MaryAnne went on, "'cause those boys have done some serious stuff."

"What kind of serious stuff?" the sheriff asked.

"The kind that puts a person in prison for forty to life."

LATER THAT EVENING, the group left Kate and Rebecca at the hospital and returned to the motel in Gatlinburg. Then sometime before midnight, the ICU nurse encouraged Kate and Rebecca to go get some rest, since they wouldn't be allowed to see Paul until morning anyway. She assured them that they'd receive a call if there was any change in Paul's status. Kate was beyond exhausted, but she didn't know if she'd be able to sleep.

"I'm so sorry, honey, that we didn't find both your father and Marcus," Kate said.

"I'm the one who should be apologizing," Rebecca insisted. "Who knows what Marcus did to cause those men to come looking for him. It's just . . ." Her words failed, then after a moment, she continued. "He could already be dead, for all we know."

"Don't talk that way," Kate admonished.

"What other reason could they have for tracking him down and kidnapping him?" Rebecca stopped to catch her breath. "When MaryAnne was talking, I remembered where I'd seen those men." Rebecca closed her eyes and a tear escaped her lashes.

Kate reached for her daughter's hand.

"When we first started dating, Marcus took me out for pizza at Bruno Brothers," she went on. "I'd gone to the ladies' room, but when I came back to the table, I saw two men talking to Marcus. They'd seemed very angry, and when I asked Marcus about it later, he got upset and told me not to worry about it. But I remember he was shaken by whatever they'd said."

"Did you suspect that Marcus was gambling?" Kate asked.

"That's the sad part." Rebecca lifted her forlorn gaze to the ceiling. "I had these niggling thoughts. He would say things." She shook her head. "Mom, he bought me a lottery ticket on our first date, and I still didn't have a clue."

"Well, it's not my idea of a romantic gift, but a lot of people do buy lottery tickets," Kate said.

But Rebecca was shaking her head. "There's more. He'd disappear for days at a time, and when I'd finally get ahold of him, I could hear a lot of commotion in the background. Don't you see? He was at the racetrack. There was always something, but I chose to stick my head in the sand. That's why it's my fault that Daddy is fighting for his life."

"None of this is your fault, honey. You can't blame yourself. Marcus made his own choices, and Daddy chose to go after him. Both decisions were out of your hands."

"But if I hadn't suggested that Marcus go along on the trip—"

"Who could've guessed that any of this would happen?" Kate lifted her daughter's chin and looked into her eyes. "You aren't responsible for other people's decisions, and we don't expect you to know the future, honey. We love you. No matter what."

Chapter Twenty-Four

All night Rebecca had tossed and turned in her bed. Her moans had awakened Kate several times, and at 5:45 AM, she'd screamed Marcus' name and shot upright.

"What is it, honey?" Kate asked as she turned on the bedside lamp.

Rebecca held her face in her hands. She rubbed her cheeks, then lifted her face to her mother. "I had a dream," she said.

"I guessed that," Kate said. "About Marcus?"

Rebecca nodded. "And the two men. Only we were in New York. They were . . ." Her voice trailed away, and she took a deep breath before continuing. "How are we going to find him now when we know those men are purposely evading us? Daddy said that Marcus was dying!"

Kate glanced at the clock, noting that the sun would be rising within the hour. She dialed search headquarters to see if the rescue team was getting ready to head out.

"Yes, ma'am," Ranger Morton said. "We'll keep searching until Marcus is found between Elkmont and Chimney Tops. But I'm afraid that since this has become a criminal investigation, we can't let civilians search anymore. It's just too dangerous."

"But . . ." Kate began to protest.

"No buts, ma'am. It's by order of the local sheriff's department. And all stations have been instructed that no car is to leave the park without first being cleared by the police."

REBECCA PACED the hospital waiting room that morning.

"At least I could *do* something before!" she complained. "Marcus could be dead already."

"Honey," Kate said, holding a cup of steaming coffee out to her. "Sit down."

"How can I be so angry with him and so devastated at the same time? Right now I'm doubting everything he ever said to me . . ." She blew out a heavy breath.

"On some level, you still care about him, even though he didn't tell you everything about himself. You'll have to sort it all out once he comes home."

"*If* he comes home," Rebecca corrected.

Just then Kate's cell phone rang. Rebecca took her coffee so that Kate could answer the call.

"Kate, it's Sheriff Roberts," he said. "I have a bit of news for you. I talked to the West Orange Police Department, and they confirmed that there's an arrest warrant out for those two Sacco men. We also ran the prints Deputy Spencer took off the stolen El Dorado. It's them all right."

"What are the warrants for?" Kate asked.

The sheriff paused as if he didn't want to tell her, then he finally said, "Racketeering and suspicion of murder."

BY NINE O'CLOCK, the Wilsons, Eli, Joe, and the Jenners joined in the wait at the hospital. MaryAnne had called earlier to say she'd wait for news of her brother at the visitor center. She was simply too nervous to be so far away from him, even though it was only a half-hour's drive.

Eli sat near Rebecca. His presence seemed to calm her tattered nerves. Joe paced the room, that walking stick of his thumping the floor with each step. Livvy had taken a spot near Kate at one of the tables that flanked the soda and candy machines.

Kate needed to do something to take her mind off Paul. She'd called Betty Anderson back in Copper Mill to update those who were praying on all that had happened. Then she'd gone to see Sam who was in a room not far from Paul's. He was thrilled to learn that they'd found Paul, though his eyes had clouded when she'd told him Paul still was unconscious.

Then when she'd gone in to see Paul, he'd looked better to her. Yet his eyes remained closed, his sunken cheeks and bruised face testifying to his weakened condition.

"Come on."

Eli's warm voice broke into Kate's musings. She glanced up to see him reaching out a hand to Rebecca.

"We're going to go for a little walk," he said to Kate.

She nodded and offered a smile, then once they'd left, she pulled her laptop from its case, set it up on the table, and turned it on.

"What are you looking up?" Livvy asked once the screen had booted up.

"I keep thinking about those men," Kate said. "They

don't know the woods any better than Marcus, from what I've heard of them. So it has me wondering . . ."

She clicked on a map of Great Smoky Mountains National Park, and when the page had downloaded, she said, "We found Paul here." She pointed to the spot halfway between the Appalachian Trail and Chimney Tops Trail, named for a pair of mountains with a chimney-like appearance.

"Does it make sense to you that the search team is starting back at Elkmont?"

By this time, Joe's interest had been piqued. He pulled up a chair on the other side of the table.

"They're coming from both directions, aren't they?" he asked.

Kate nodded. "I understand coming from the south; it's close by where we found Paul. But the kidnappers aren't going to be able to survive in the wilderness that long, not if they have an injured man with them. And from what Paul managed to say yesterday, Marcus is on the brink. Unless . . ."—she paused to think—"unless they aren't expecting to keep caring for him."

Kate glanced around the room. Justin and James were playing games on their handheld electronic toys while Danny read a magazine. Kate glanced at James, thankful that he seemed to have worked out his differences with his parents.

"Meaning?" Livvy asked, pulling Kate's attention back to the task at hand.

"Once they get what they want from Marcus, they'll dump him, leave him for dead," Kate said.

"What is it they want, then?" Joe leaned forward, his bald forehead furrowed in thought.

Just then the ICU nurse poked her head in the door. Everyone turned to hear what she had to report.

"Mrs. Hanlon?" she said, an expectant expression on her face.

"Yes." Kate rose to her feet and met the woman's gaze, her heart suddenly thumping in her chest as she anticipated what she was going to say.

"Your husband is awake."

Chapter Twenty-Five

Paul was sitting up in bed drinking juice through a straw when Kate and the others entered the room. She'd immediately called Rebecca's cell with the news, so she and Eli were close behind.

"Where you been?" Paul asked, a grin spreading across his battered face.

Kate laughed, even as tears of relief fell down her cheeks. He pulled her into an embrace. Though his arms were weak, he held on tight. Kate closed her eyes and whispered a prayer of thanks that Paul was okay. When she pulled back, he wiped the tears from her cheeks and smiled into her eyes. How she loved this man!

Rebecca was waiting in line for her hug.

"Daddy, we were so scared," she said as he held her.

"*Shh,*" he said. "I'm not going anywhere." Then he brushed a strand of hair from her face and kissed her forehead.

The rest gathered at the foot of Paul's bed. He paused to gaze at each face, and Kate reached for his hand.

"Did they find Marcus?" Paul asked.

"No." Rebecca shook her head. "Search and rescue are looking, but still no word."

"What exactly happened?" Joe Tucker asked. "How did you get yourself into this mess?"

Paul chuckled at the question, then shook his head. "I'm not completely sure, Joe!" he began, then looked at Rebecca. "Marcus had been so shaken after that mountain man pointed the gun at him, I was afraid he'd do something crazy. I'd never seen anyone so on edge. He kept looking around like someone was following him. Then when he took off, I felt instinctively that it was no pleasure hike. He'd taken his backpack, so I grabbed mine." He shrugged. "Then when I saw the bear tracks and his pack all torn up, I was terrified of what could've happened to him."

"When did you finally catch up with him?" Eli asked.

Paul scratched his head. "The days got a little confused, so I don't remember if it was the second day or the third. I think it was the second. Right after the rainstorm. Wow, that was some storm!"

Kate squeezed his hand, remembering her fear for him during that time.

"There's nothing like being in the middle of a big lightning storm without a tent," Paul said. "The wind was howling, and the rain came down in sheets. If I hadn't been in the situation I was in, I would've rather enjoyed it, I think." He paused and grinned at Kate. "I'll have you know I still remember how to start a fire with a flint."

"But you had matches, didn't you?" Kate recalled the waterproof ones he'd packed.

"Left them at camp," Paul said. "I wished I'd had those iodine tablets too. Remember I left them on the dresser?"

Kate felt bad that she'd told him not to take them, and Paul squeezed her hand before changing the subject.

"Marcus broke his arm pretty bad. I splinted it, but . . ." —his eyes darkened, and he lifted his gaze to Rebecca— "he had a fever, honey. To be honest, I don't think he was conscious when those men took him." He turned to Kate. "They were the same men we saw at the Bristol."

Kate nodded. "We were trying to reach you," she said, "to warn you that something wasn't right. We saw those men on Sunday snooping around Marcus' rental car in front of the diner, and then they showed up at the house driving a stolen vehicle and claiming that Marcus was missing."

"Missing?" Paul repeated. "So, why would they kidnap Marcus . . . and beat me up in the process?" He rubbed his bandaged forehead.

"We have ideas," Kate said. "Marcus' sister told us they're loan sharks. And Sheriff Roberts said they're wanted for racketeering and suspicion of murder."

A look of fear filled Paul's eyes. "So, that's why Marcus freaked out like he did. He didn't want anyone to find him, and when I finally did find him, he kept saying things about making sure Rebecca was safe." He glanced at their daughter, and Kate saw her composure crumble.

"Do you have any idea where they took him?" Joe stayed focused. "Did you hear them say anything?"

Paul shook his head. "I don't have a clue. But Marcus wasn't doing well; I know that much. He'd been too cold for too long. He was acting really out of it. We'd stopped and camped for the night at the lean-to, then he had a fever that morning. He was burning up. I was afraid maybe he had an infection." He took a deep breath before going on. "I'd tried to go get help, but then I was worried about him, so I turned back. I'd covered him with my survival blanket, but without sunlight, those things don't do all that much. I was getting so worried that he'd . . . die." His gaze flicked to Kate, and she patted his hand. "He seemed to be giving up. But when I got back to the lean-to, I saw the men there. At first I thought they were rescuers. They had the orange vests on. But the way they were talking . . . I just knew they weren't there for good reasons. I confronted them and . . ."—he gingerly touched the bandaged spot on the back of his head—"A lot of good it did me. I got a few decent punches in, but without any real food or rest, I just didn't have the strength to help Marcus."

He turned to Rebecca and lifted her chin. "We'll keep praying for him, honey. God knows where he is and if anyone can rescue Marcus, he can," he said.

Her woe-filled expression tugged at Kate's heart.

"It might be too late already, Daddy."

Chapter Twenty-Six

Paul may as well have been Lazarus, as quickly as he recovered from his ordeal. By noon he had been moved to a regular room and he was eating food again, though it was of the soft variety. His color had returned, and his skin began to regain some of its elasticity. The doctors confirmed that there was no permanent damage from the dehydration, and his temperature was at a perfect 98.6.

He was slurping Jell-O when a familiar voice at the door said, "Knock, knock."

Paul and Kate turned to see Sam Gorman in the doorway. He was dressed in jeans and a wool shirt. His thick brown hair was combed back as if he were on his way to a high-school dance.

"Sam!" Paul said. "Come on in!"

He came into the room and shook his friend's hand.

"Can't tell you how glad I am that you're okay," he said.

"That goes double for me," Paul replied. "Kate told me you were trying to have a heart attack."

Sam waved the comment away. "I'm just dandy," he said. "The doctor put me on a low-fat, low-salt, low-taste diet.

We'll see how long that lasts." He laughed and grinned at Paul. "I'm about to head home with the others, but I had to see you for myself before I took off."

"I hope I won't be far behind you," Paul said. "And maybe they'll find Marcus before then."

"I wish there was something I could do," Sam said.

"You can keep praying," Kate suggested. "Never enough of that to go around."

Sam nodded, looking at Paul. "That I can. Our prayers for you paid off, now, didn't they? With you sitting here and looking well." Sam's expression turned serious. "I can't tell you how hard it was, to have my good friend missing. I'm glad you're back."

They said their good-byes, and Sam quietly shut the door behind him. Livvy and her men stopped in a little later, along with Joe and the Wilsons. Now that they were no longer allowed to help in the search for Marcus, it seemed the time had arrived to head back home. They offered words of farewell and thankfulness that Paul was on the mend.

As the men went ahead to load up the rusted fifteen-passenger van that had brought them to the Smokies, Livvy lingered with Kate in the hallway outside Paul's room.

"I can't tell you how much it meant to have you with me this week," Kate said.

"I was just going to say the same thing. And I wanted to thank you for all your help with James. I can see that his ordeal has opened him up to us in a new way. I didn't realize that he'd started to shut us out; it happened so gradually." She paused and smiled into Kate's eyes. "Anyway, thanks for everything."

The two women embraced, and a tear streamed down Kate's cheek.

"See," Livvy said, "I told you we wouldn't leave until Paul was safe."

"Thank you," Kate said.

Livvy turned to go, and Kate watched until she disappeared around a corner. Then as she opened the door to her husband's room, her cell phone rang. She fumbled in her handbag, making a mental note to invest in a smaller one, then hit the TALK button. "This is Kate."

"Kate, it's Sheriff Roberts."

"What is it? Have you found him?" Kate asked as she exchanged a worried look with Paul.

"No, Kate. Sorry. But we did find the other car, the one they took from Willy's Bait and Tackle."

Kate inhaled sharply.

"There were ransom notes," the sheriff said. "Looked like rough drafts of something they may plan to send to the authorities. We're thinking that may be their plan, and why they're trying to get Marcus out of the mountains. It's a theory, but it's the best we've got."

"Ransom?" Kate said in disbelief.

Paul shifted in his bed, waiting and watching as Kate listened.

"Does MaryAnne know?" Kate asked.

"She's here with me," the sheriff said, "so, yes, she's aware of the situation."

"Would their family pay if—?" Kate began.

"I've advised them not to, but we aren't quite at that point yet," he reminded her.

"Of course," she said.

When Kate closed her phone, she was puzzled. Ransom? Something about that just didn't seem right to her. As she thought about it, she realized what it was. MaryAnne had said they'd known the Sacco brothers since childhood. She said that if that were true, the brothers would have known that Marcus wasn't a person of means. Had they simply been grasping at straws, or had they chased Marcus here in hopes of finding someone who would cover his gambling debts for him? And if so, from whom could they demand payment?

Paul was studying her face, obviously waiting for her to fill him in on the details. "Ransom?" he asked with a raised eyebrow.

"They found a stolen car belonging to Willy Bergren and ransom notes inside," Kate began.

Just then, Eli and Rebecca came in from another walk. Eli was carrying a large black bag.

"Hey, Daddy," Rebecca said, bending to kiss her father on the cheek. Then she glanced at her mother. "What's wrong?" she asked, obviously reading the expression on Kate's face.

"Sheriff Roberts just called to say they found the car the men stole from Copper Mill."

"Oh?" Rebecca glanced at Eli. "Was that all he had to say?"

Kate shook her head. "There were ransom notes in the car," she went on, "but they were only rough drafts. We aren't positive that's what they were actually planning."

Rebecca took a chair as if she needed a rest to let the news soak in.

"So ... um," Eli said, pointing over his shoulder toward the door, "The guys dropped off Paul's camping gear ... Where would you like me to put it?"

"In the trunk of my car," Kate said. "I'll go down with you. I want to get a soda from the machine anyway." She glanced at Rebecca, who was still trying to comprehend the news. "You stay here with Daddy, okay?"

Rebecca nodded.

Eli and Kate walked toward the Honda that was parked in the visitor's lot. They hadn't said anything to each other since they left the room, and Kate wondered what was on the young man's mind. He kept glancing at her and chewing his lower lip as if he was nervous.

"I have to tell you, Kate," he finally said, "I really like your daughter."

Kate glanced at him, and a blush immediately flamed across his face. "I didn't mean it like that ..." He cleared his throat.

"How did you mean it, Eli?" Kate teased. Then she said seriously, "I think she likes you too. She's needed a friend in all of this."

"Yeah"—his head bobbed up and down—"a friend. She must really care about Marcus."

"Sure she does," Kate said, "but you never know with those actors."

He smiled shyly at her as they reached the car. Kate unlocked the trunk and tugged it open. Looking inside, she was surprised to see Marcus' black suitcase sitting there. She had forgotten that Rebecca had brought it along when they'd first left Copper Mill. She began to move it to the side to make room for Paul's bag, when a thought occurred to her.

After the Sacco brothers had been to the house, it looked as if Marcus' suitcase had been rummaged through. Kate had assumed the brothers had done it, but was starting to wonder if maybe they weren't the ones who had stolen Rebecca's ring after all. She remembered the way Marcus had talked about the heirloom, the way he'd seemed eager to see it and know its value. What if the men hadn't taken the ring, she considered, but instead, Marcus had taken it to pay back his gambling debt?

Her gaze traveled to Eli as if the thought had been so loud, he might have heard it too.

He looked at her curiously. "You okay, Kate?"

"Can you get that other bag out?" she said.

He shrugged and lifted the black suitcase to the ground. Kate immediately bent to unzip it. Piece by piece, she emptied the suitcase, examining each article carefully. Then she checked every side pocket and inside pocket. There was nothing.

Eli squatted next to her and asked, "What are we looking for?"

"Rebecca's ring," she said.

He sat back in obvious shock.

Then she noticed that the suitcase had a false bottom, with a layer of nylon Velcroed on top of another. She peeled it away, and there taped to the outside section of the suitcase was the sapphire-and-diamond ring.

Chapter Twenty-Seven

B y Sunday morning, the doctors were ready to release Paul from the hospital. He was still thin, and he hadn't regained all of his strength, but he was well enough to finish his recuperation at home.

"I think I should stay at the motel with Marcus' sister," Rebecca announced. "I can't just leave Marcus out there, without . . ." She shrugged and glanced at Eli, who was leaning against the windowsill.

Kate was thankful that he'd been with them through everything. Even when everyone else had headed back to Copper Mill the day before, he had remained. Kate knew it was because of his growing affection for Rebecca, and yet she also knew that her daughter was confused and vulnerable.

"After all Marcus has done," Rebecca went on, "I still don't want anything to happen to him."

She looked frail, as if she might shatter. There hadn't been any new developments on the search for Marcus, despite the discovery of the kidnappers' stolen car and the ransom notes. The impression Kate got when she'd last spoken to Sheriff Roberts was that this was their last chance to find him. If they didn't, they would announce that they were halting operations the following day. So far, the search area had simply proven to be too vast and the kidnappers too conniving.

"Honey, I understand that you feel responsible to stay here for Marcus, and you can make your own choices. But I think you might need us right now." Kate placed a comforting hand on Rebecca's arm. "There's nothing you can do for Marcus that isn't already being done. And to be honest, honey, we need you too."

Rebecca fell into her mother's arms, crying, yet visibly relieved. "I needed to hear that," she said on an exhaled breath. "I do need you."

So it was settled. Rebecca would leave the wilderness and Marcus behind.

THE DRIVE BACK to Copper Mill was pleasant enough. Kate drove, while Paul slept in the backseat with Eli beside him. Rebecca rode shotgun. She'd been quiet most of the ride, and Kate could only guess that she was thinking about Marcus and everything that had happened during the past week.

The panorama of autumn spread before them as they crested each hill, then dipped into shaded tunnels of color. The road turned south, and Kate flipped on the radio to a classical station, allowing the lull of the music to ease the stress in her body.

She had been thinking about the ring. She glanced at it on Rebecca's hand. Did the Sacco brothers know about it and its value? New thoughts began to formulate: Had Marcus told them about it? Perhaps he had promised it to them before he and Rebecca left New York. She couldn't know the answer to that question, but it tugged at her.

She assumed the Sacco brothers had looked through the suitcase at the house. But she wondered if they had assumed that Marcus had already taken the ring, and perhaps was running from them, when they couldn't find it. If they had known about its existence and had been unable to find it, that would explain why they'd gone after Marcus in the woods. But what would they do with Marcus once they discovered that the ring wasn't on him? Leave him for dead? The thought chilled her. Would they think Marcus had been lying to them all along? The men were already wanted for suspicion of murder. She pictured Paul, so beaten up by the two brutes.

She remembered the slip of paper with their home address scratched on it.

A sick feeling came over her as her intuition kicked into high gear.

They had found Marcus in the woods . . . without the ring. And Marcus didn't know his suitcase had been moved to Gatlinburg.

Kate pressed on the accelerator, and Rebecca jolted in her seat. "What's going on, Mom?"

"I know where they are."

Chapter Twenty-Eight

There were no police cars in sight when Kate drove past the house. She'd called the Copper Mill dispatcher only to be told that Deputy Spencer was out on an emergency call and that reinforcements from Pine Ridge would come just as soon as they could. She wished Sheriff Roberts was back in town, but he was still in the Smokies looking for Marcus. The dispatcher had promised that they'd hurry.

An old sedan was parked in the driveway. Kate assumed it was probably another stolen vehicle. Livvy's car, that she'd left parked in the Hanlons' driveway all week, was gone. No doubt the Jenners had come to pick it up when they'd returned home the previous day.

"What should we do?" Eli asked from the backseat.

"We should wait for the police," Paul answered, now fully awake.

"Unless they try to get away," Rebecca said.

Kate glanced in the rearview mirror and saw the disapproving look on her husband's face.

"Marcus could be in there, in danger, honey," Kate reminded him.

Paul nodded his head. "Exactly. These men are dangerous."

Kate drove a good half mile up the road, still well out of sight of the house, and pulled a U-turn. As the car crawled slowly back up the road, her heart thumped in her chest, and sweat beaded on her forehead.

"Mom, I'm really scared," Rebecca said.

"It's going to be okay." Kate patted her daughter's knee, then slowly pressed the accelerator. She didn't want to confront these men; she just wanted to make sure they stayed put until the police arrived.

Kate edged her Honda closer to the house. She pulled to a stop alongside the road, put the car into park, and shut off the engine. Then she reached for her cell phone and dialed the dispatcher again.

"Copper Mill dispatch," the operator said.

"Hello, this is Kate Hanlon. I called a little bit ago about those kidnappers," she said.

"Yes, ma'am," the female voice said.

"We're at the house, or at least up the road from it. I can see a car parked there."

"Do you know for sure that people are in the house?" the dispatcher asked.

Kate unbuckled her seat belt and opened the door.

"Where are you going?" the others said almost in unison.

Kate waved a hand. "I won't get too close. I need a better view."

She climbed out, Eli close at her heels. She'd heard him tell Rebecca and Paul to stay put. Then she heard the sound of keys jingling. She glanced back to see that Eli had pulled the keys from the ignition.

She gave him a curious look and held the cell phone to her ear as she crossed the ditch on the other side of the road and edged toward the woods that bordered their property.

"I can see the back of the house," she told the dispatcher as she moved brush aside and tiptoed to the woods' edge, where she had a clear view of their backyard.

"Is this the house key?" Eli held up the gold-plated key.

Kate nodded and placed a hand over the mouthpiece. "Why?" she asked.

"Don't worry about it," he said.

"Hello?" the dispatcher's voice pulled Kate back. "What's going on?"

"The sliding-glass door is wide open," Kate whispered. "Wait."

She couldn't believe her eyes. Eli was racing down the ditch alongside the road. His head was down, his shoulders hunched as he ran. Then he dropped, flat on his belly, when he was parallel with the house. She watched in stunned silence as he edged up onto the side lawn and around to the front, where she lost sight of him.

Panic filled her as she wondered what those men would do if they caught Eli inside the house. She watched for what felt like an eternity, but there was no movement.

Then finally, the taller man came out. He was cursing loudly.

"I can see them," Kate whispered to the dispatcher.

"Serves him right," the second one said as he shut the sliding-glass door. He slammed his fist against the side of the house, and Kate felt herself jump. Where was Eli? She scanned the property, hoping for a glimpse of him, but there was nothing. The men headed for the front of the house, and Kate followed at a distance.

"They're leaving!" Kate said to the dispatcher as she watched them climb into the car. "Where are the police?"

"They should be there soon, Mrs. Hanlon. Just stay on the line."

The car roared to life and backed out of the driveway.

Kate ran back to the Honda and got in, then realized that Eli had her keys. She could do nothing but wait until Eli emerged from the house. Thankfully, within only seconds, Eli walked outside shaking his head.

She handed the phone to Rebecca to talk to the dispatcher. The Sacco brothers were already moving at a good clip toward town along Smoky Mountain Road.

"He's not there," Eli said, pulling the car door closed behind him and handing the keys to Kate. She put the car in gear and hit the accelerator.

"They're almost at that next house," Rebecca told the dispatcher.

Kate was surprised at the calmness of her daughter's voice when she spoke. The distant sound of sirens echoed from the west. Kate steered around a bend in the mountainous road, trying to keep up without alerting the men to their presence.

She glanced at Rebecca, whose eyes were as big as dinner plates.

"So if Marcus wasn't in the house, where is he?" she asked.

"I didn't see him in the house, but that doesn't mean he isn't in the car," Eli said.

"They're coming up to the high school," Rebecca said into the phone. "They're turning west on Mountain Laurel Road."

The sirens grew louder, though Kate still couldn't spot exactly where they were. She followed the sedan around the corner, punching the accelerator once she'd cleared the intersection. The men were going at least seventy now. No doubt they'd heard the sirens too.

Then she saw them. Two police cars were coming from the west, with a blockade behind them. Smith and Sweetwater Streets were both shut off by police cars with lights circling and officers at the ready.

"We see the police," Rebecca told the dispatcher. Then to Kate, "She said to pull over, Mom. The police will take it from here."

Kate did as instructed, then watched as the stolen car attempted to drive north on Smith Street. The police were on it immediately. The car stopped and the police officers opened the doors, guns drawn, and told the men to get out with their hands in the air. The officers forced them to the ground and put them in handcuffs.

Kate, Rebecca, and Eli were out of the car and running toward the men.

"We're going to take these two down to HQ right away," a heavyset officer informed Kate when they arrived.

Rebecca was frantically looking inside the stolen car.

"Wait! They know where Marcus is!" she said, her voice rising with each word as she marched over. "We don't have time for all that! He could be dead for all we know!"

She turned to the taller of the two suspects.

"Where did you take him?" she shouted.

"Lady, I don't know who you're talkin' about," he said.

"Liar!" she shouted even louder. "You kidnapped Marcus! Where is he?" She looked at the smaller one. He shifted where he lay on the ground and his pale eyes gazed into Kate's.

One of the policemen pulled the smaller man to his feet, then asked. "What's all this about a kidnapping? I thought it was a breaking and entering."

"They're wanted on suspicion of kidnapping," Kate informed him. "They abducted my daughter's . . . friend in the Smoky Mountains."

A light of recognition went on. "I heard about that." He turned to the stocky one and then to the taller one and quickly read them their Miranda rights. Then he said, "Tell us where he is. If he's alive, there might be a chance the judge will be lenient, but if not, you're looking at a real long time behind bars. A *real* long time."

The stocky guy's face twisted. He looked at his brother, who shook his head and glared at him.

"I . . . ," he began.

"Jerry!" the other scolded. "What are you doin'?"

"It was your fault it took us so long to get here. If you hadn't made so many pit stops, they never would've caught us. Do you want to sit in prison your whole life, just because the boss . . ." His words trailed off when the tall one hissed at him not to say another word.

"Do it for yourself," Kate appealed to Jerry. "Let your brother go to prison, but save yourself. Don't let Marcus die out there."

"We didn't mean for any of this to happen," the man began, meeting Kate's eye. "We'd been tailin' him in the city all week, but then he took off. If he'd just paid up, none of this would've happened."

His brother snapped. "Stop yer blabbin'!"

"Do you want Mack to die out there? Do ya, Alex? It wasn't supposed to come to this. I don't want to go to jail."

The officer leaned next to him and spoke in hushed tones. The taller one struggled to break free, and two other officers held him down. "You can't do this!" he screamed.

"I've got to," Jerry said.

Finally the officer who had been talking to the smaller one said, "We have a location." He ran to his squad car to radio it in to the Gatlinburg authorities.

The suspects were placed in a police car for the time being. Several long minutes later, the officer returned to Kate and the others.

"They need the one Sacco brother to show them exactly where your friend is," the officer announced. "He's agreed to do it."

"I want to come too," Rebecca said. She looked at her mother. "I need to, Mom."

Kate saw the fear in her daughter's face.

"Can we both go?" Kate asked.

The officer nodded. "Having trustworthy witnesses will be key, since we can't trust these idiots as far as we can throw 'em. A chopper should be here shortly."

ELI PROMISED KATE he would get Paul set up at home, and if they needed him to come get them once they found Marcus, he'd gladly do that. She squeezed the young man's hand, so thankful for his care. She then leaned into the backseat and gave Paul a hug. He looked exhausted from all the excitement.

"You going to be okay?" she asked.

"I'll be fine," he whispered. Then he kissed her and told her to be careful.

Worry edged into Kate's mind. What if Marcus was already dead? The man had said they'd left him at a bald just south of Huskey Gap. But that was quite a hike away from where Paul had been found. Paul had said that Marcus had been hanging on by a thread already. What had two more days out in the elements done to the man's already failing health?

Within half an hour, the rhythmic *thwop* of helicopter blades sounded from the north. The Pine Ridge medical chopper had been called in for the emergency trip. It swooped in to land in the middle of the intersection of Mountain Laurel Road and Sweetwater Street. Kate and

Rebecca ran toward it as the redheaded officer brought the smaller Sacco brother along.

Kate and Rebecca's hair blew uncontrollably as they climbed into the chopper and fastened their seat belts. Two others, whom Kate assumed were EMTs, were already on board. They gave nods all around since it was too loud to hear verbal greetings. The pilot turned to give a thumbs-up, and they lifted into the air.

The vehicles and people on the roads grew smaller as they rose into the sky. The chopper tilted to the northeast, and the ground beneath them hurried past. As they approached the mountains, the vastness of the Smokies overwhelmed Kate. How had they thought they could find anyone in that wilderness? That they found Paul was a miracle in itself. She lifted a prayer of profound thanks.

Her thoughts turned to Marcus as she prayed. How many nights had the young man spent in the cold mountains? One day had slipped into the next during this nightmare, and she could only imagine how much worse it had been for him. Rebecca reached for her mother's hand, and Kate gave it a squeeze. Their eyes met, and tears streamed down the pretty girl's face. She looked so tired.

"We'll find him," Kate mouthed.

Rebecca nodded, then turned her gaze out the window.

Kate glanced across the helicopter at the weaselly little man in handcuffs. He looked to be in his early thirties. He was staring at the floor. Then he'd squint his eyes in a nervous way and lift his face to the ceiling. Kate pitied the young man and wondered how he'd come to this sad state.

After another hour, the chopper began its descent. It skimmed the trees, and Kate was afraid of crashing, but then a clearing appeared out of nowhere, and the pilot gently set the machine down.

When they exited the craft, its blades still moving, Kate didn't see Marcus. The short man led the way with the officer and EMTs right behind. Rebecca must have spotted Marcus then, because she ran on ahead toward a rhododendron bush that bordered a flat boulder.

There he lay, motionless. His skin was blue. Kate had never seen a living person that color before in her life.

Chapter Twenty-Nine

The emergency medical crew took over immediately. One man examined Marcus' eyes while the other felt for a pulse. Kate and Rebecca stood back while they worked. Kate held her breath, then let it out when the man turned to Rebecca with a smile.

"We have a pulse," he said.

The police officer and the other EMT brought up the gurney to transport Marcus to the chopper. Rebecca reached out to touch his hand but pulled back immediately.

"He's so cold!" she said. She pressed her fingers to her cheeks, and Kate could see the fear in her eyes.

Kate sent up a prayer—no, a myriad of prayers all at once—that Marcus' heart would beat strongly, that the blankets they were wrapping him in would begin to warm him right away, that he would make it to the hospital in time. She prayed for Rebecca too, that her daughter wouldn't fall apart, that she'd be strong and courageous.

Finally Marcus' body was lifted onto the gurney, and they rushed him to the waiting helicopter. The policeman and one of the EMTs climbed aboard to guide the gurney up into the craft, while the other steadied it.

Kate was barely buckled in when the chopper began to lift skyward.

Rebecca moved to Marcus' side, kneeling on the floor of the helicopter next to him and stroking his dark hair. The medical personnel were hooking him up to an IV and checking his vitals, but they didn't seem to mind her presence. His eyes were still closed. Rebecca lightly touched his cheek that had a week's worth of beard on it, but he didn't move.

When they finally landed at the Fort Sanders Sevier Medical Center, Kate felt a sense of impending doom. Marcus had been unresponsive throughout the flight. At one point, the EMTs had even started doing chest compressions and squeezing an air bag to help him breathe. She stood back with Rebecca and watched him being wheeled into the hospital. Then they turned to see the police officer lead the suspect away.

"All this time," Rebecca turned to Kate, "all our hard work to find him, all our prayers . . . and he's still going to die!" She broke into deep, wracking sobs as Kate held her.

Kate smoothed her hair and spoke soft prayers into her daughter's ear. Finally, when Rebecca had calmed herself, they walked into the white corridor that led to the ER waiting room. There was no sight of Marcus or those who had brought him in, but his sister, MaryAnne, was there in the waiting room, looking frightened and alone. Rebecca hugged her and Kate patted her shoulder.

"They didn't say anything to me about how he is," MaryAnne said. "They just called and said they'd found him."

"He's fighting for his life." Rebecca took the woman's hand as they sat on padded chairs. "He definitely has hypothermia, and I'm sure he's dehydrated. And his pulse was pretty weak . . . But at least he's alive!"

Kate sat down and prayed with the women for a few minutes, then she told MaryAnne what had happened to Marcus.

When Kate had finished, she shook her head. "How did he get into something like this?" she asked, looking from Kate to Rebecca. "He's a good kid. He really is."

"Everyone has their weaknesses," Kate said. "Little by little, we allow our defenses to be chipped away." Then she gave MaryAnne a sympathetic look. "I can't imagine how hard this is for you."

The heavyset woman lifted her eyes to the ceiling. "He has to make it through," she said. "I don't know how our mother would handle it if he died."

The local news channel was droning on the elevated TV in the corner, when Kate's attention was drawn to a female reporter who had just come on the air.

". . . In Gatlinburg, that second lost hiker has been found. We don't have any additional information at this time. The hiker who has been missing since last Monday in Smoky Mountain National Park has been found. His condition is still unknown."

Kate clicked the remote off and glanced at Rebecca. "News travels fast," she said.

Excusing herself, she walked outside and pulled out her phone to call Paul. It rang several times before Eli picked it up.

"Hanlon residence," Eli said.

"Eli, it's Kate. Is Paul awake?"

"He just lay down," Eli said. "Do you want me to wake him?"

"No. He needs his rest. You can tell him when he gets up."

"So?"

"We found Marcus." She could hear Eli's sigh of relief. "But," she went on, "he's hanging onto life by a thread. They were doing chest compressions when we got to the hospital, and they've been working on him ever since. We haven't gotten an update." She glanced at her watch, realizing it was past suppertime.

"Deputy Spencer called here," Eli said.

"What did he say?"

"He wanted to get statements from you and Rebecca. I asked him what the one Sacco brother had to say."

"Did he confess?"

"No, but there's no doubt that they came for Rebecca's ring. When it wasn't at the house, they decided that Marcus had taken it." Then he paused and added, "Are you going to press charges against Marcus?"

"I don't want to even think about that right now," Kate said. "We just want him to live. He's been through enough this week."

"How's Rebecca holding up?" Eli asked.

"She's okay."

She heard the pause in his response, as if he'd hoped to hear more about her. "Well," he said. "Let me know when you hear more about Marcus, okay? I'll tell Paul as soon as he wakes up."

Shortly after Kate made her way back to the waiting room, a doctor brought news about Marcus. "He has a broken arm, but he's breathing on his own now and his heart is beating okay. He'll be in the ICU for a while. We're working to bring up his core temperature and rehydrate him. But since he's still unconscious, we don't know the extent of damage to his organs."

A nurse escorted MaryAnne up to ICU to sit with her brother. When she returned, she gave Kate and Rebecca the number of Marcus' room.

They took the elevator to the ICU floor and slowly entered the room. Kate nodded to the nurse who was attending to him. The woman adjusted the fluids in his IV, placed his chart back on its hook, turned the lights to a more relaxed setting, and left.

Rebecca pulled a chair alongside the bed and gazed at him. His sunken eyes were closed and rimmed in dark circles, but some of the color had returned to his cheeks. He looked thin, very thin. Rebecca touched one of his hands lightly, as if not wanting to disturb him. His other arm was in a sling, and heated blankets surrounded him. Rebecca glanced up at the monitor that kept rhythm with his heart. From what Kate could tell, it seemed like a strong heart-beat, though she was hardly a medical expert. She was thankful to see the rise and fall of his chest.

They sat in silence for a few minutes, then Kate heard the door open and turned her head as the doctor entered the room. His name tag read "Dr. McCoy."

"I'm sorry to interrupt," he said. He picked up the file and looked through it.

The white-haired man gazed at Marcus thoughtfully and said, "You're lucky he's still here. If you'd found him any later—"

"When do you think he'll wake up?" Rebecca asked.

"Hard to tell, though I don't expect it will be long now. He's had four bags of fluids, and his temp is close to nor-mal." He smiled kindly, then took out his otoscope and looked into Marcus' eyes and ears. Next he listened to Marcus' heart and lungs with his stethoscope. He also looked at the IV bags that hung from the tree-on-wheels alongside the bed, then wrote something on the chart.

"Are you the girlfriend?" The doctor smiled at Rebecca.

"Well, I . . ." Rebecca began to reply, but then said, "No."

When their fifteen minutes were up, they returned to the waiting room, and MaryAnne went back to ICU to sit with Marcus a little while longer.

Kate put an arm around her daughter's shoulders as they walked outside for a little fresh air. "What are you thinking?" she asked.

Rebecca was quiet for a moment, thoughtful. Then she said, "I was thinking of the first time I met Marcus. That gorgeous smile, those hazel eyes that pulled me in. He could melt my heart." She shook her head, then went on. "Then I started asking myself all these questions. Why hadn't he confided in me? Why hadn't he been able to tell me about what was going on? And, of course, the most difficult question of all: did I ever know the real Marcus?"

They stood outside as the quiet of evening was just descending. The setting sun had left a trail of gold along the horizon.

"Did he lie when he told me he loved me? Not that that even matters anymore. What kind of love was it anyway if it was based on lies?" She shook her head, and Kate waited for her to go on.

"And then I thought about Eli. He isn't as handsome as Marcus is, but he's a solid, wonderful person. His faith in God pours out of him naturally . . . Marcus is always so reluctant to talk about God."

She looked her mother in the eyes, then she laughed. "I can even hear your voice echoing in my head. I've been so blind, Mom. Marcus wasn't the only one fooling me. I've been fooling myself all this time."

As Kate listened to her daughter, a deep joy welled up inside her.

KATE AND REBECCA had rented a car and were just settling into their motel room when Kate's cell phone rang.

"Hello? Mrs. Hanlon?" MaryAnne said when Kate picked it up.

"Hi, MaryAnne," Kate said. "Is everything all right?"

"The ICU nurses' station called," she said. "Marcus just woke up."

Kate gasped and turned to Rebecca. She thanked MaryAnne and promised her that they'd be right there.

"What is it?" Rebecca asked.

"Marcus is awake." She picked up her handbag and car keys from the dresser.

"I'm scared, Mom," Rebecca confessed as they hurried to their rental car. "So much has changed in the past week."

"Everything's going to be okay," Kate assured her.

KATE REACHED for her daughter's hand as they waited for the elevator to take them to the ICU floor. When they reached the floor, the doors opened, and they made their way to Marcus' room.

He was sitting up with MaryAnne beside him. His eyes were sunken orbs, and he was so thin and frail looking. Rebecca rushed to him, and he reached for her with his good arm.

"I was so worried!" she cried.

"I'm sorry," he murmured. "I'm so sorry. It was all my fault. Did you find your dad?"

Rebecca wiped the wetness from her cheeks. "Two days ago. That's how we knew you'd been kidnapped . . ." She let the sentence fall away.

Kate went to stand with MaryAnne, not wanting to intrude, yet knowing that her daughter needed her support.

Marcus' lower lip began to tremble, and his body shook as the terror of it all seemed to come over him. "I've been an idiot," he confessed. "I thought I was protecting you, but I just made things worse. And your dad . . . He was so kind to me, and what did he get in return?"

He raised his eyes to Rebecca's. She reached for a tissue and wiped his tears.

"I thought I could beat this . . . gambling addiction." He said the words with disdain. "But it's only gotten worse."

He turned to Kate, a look of gratitude in his eyes.

"I would've died without your husband. You need to know that, Mrs. Hanlon. I flipped out. I was so paranoid, I just started to run. But he tracked me down and got me food and water. He even bandaged my arm after I fell and broke it." He held up the cast-encased limb. "And then he left to get help . . . I was so weak . . . And then they came for me . . . And I couldn't run . . ."

"You need to calm down." Rebecca tenderly touched his cheek, and Marcus' eyes darted to the door. "It's over now, Marcus. The Sacco brothers are in jail."

"They are?"

"The police caught up with them earlier today. First they came to Mom and Dad's house on Sunday asking about you, and then they showed up at the park, posing as members of the search-and-rescue team."

"Oh, Mrs. Hanlon," Marcus said. "I'm so sorry I brought all this trouble into your lives. It was my own stupidity.

But I want to change," he continued. "Your husband convinced me that I *can* change." Then he turned to Rebecca.

Rebecca placed her face in her hands and took a deep breath. Kate could tell she was trying to compose herself.

"I don't know, Marcus. You lied to me," she said. "You didn't even tell me your real name. I don't know what's true and what isn't anymore."

"Marcus is my name," he said. "I changed it when I moved to New York. It's my stage name, but I did have it legally changed from Mack to Marcus. I was just so ashamed of the gambling. I thought if I could get it under control, I wouldn't have to tell you about it, because it would be in the past."

"But it's not in the past, is it, Marcus?" Her voice broke.

"I can't lose you, Becky. I'm going to beat it, I promise."

Rebecca was shaking her head. "No, Marcus. This isn't something you can do for me. It's something you have to do for yourself, without me as your motivator. It won't last if you do it for me."

"No!" Marcus said. "It'll last. I promise you."

"Promise yourself." Her tone had become calm now, almost placid, and Kate marveled at the maturity she saw in her daughter. "I never got to know the real Marcus, and maybe you've never known him either." She shrugged. "But I think you need to work this out between yourself and God. I can't help you." She stood then, as if to go.

"Don't leave me," he pleaded.

"Marcus, I care about you, and in my heart, I know you're going to be okay. But you and me, that's not going to

work. And it's okay. Your sister is here to take care of you."
She glanced at MaryAnne. "You'll be in good hands, but I
need to take care of me right now. I hope you understand
that."

Marcus slumped back against his pillows, a look of
defeat in his eyes. "I've lost everything!" he cried.

"No"—Rebecca placed a comforting hand on his
shoulder—"you're just beginning to find something. And
you know," she went on, "I'd stick with the acting. You'll
win an Oscar someday."

Chapter Thirty

Copper Mill had never looked so wonderful to Kate. Many leaves had fallen from the trees, creating an autumn carpet across the landscape, but the foothills were still vibrant, glowing in the morning light.

Kate glanced at Rebecca as they made their way through the winding hills that overlooked the quaint town.

They had left Marcus at the hospital with his sister the night before and returned to the motel for what had turned out to be the most restful night's sleep they'd had in a long time. The ICU doctor had told them that Marcus would likely be released by Tuesday or Wednesday. Rebecca had simply nodded and thanked the doctor for taking care of him.

The next morning, they checked out of their motel and headed for home, driving the car they had rented. Rebecca had been quiet as they drove, and Kate wasn't sure if her silence was regret or simple contemplation. But she knew better than to pry.

There was something about an ordeal of this magnitude that brought the rest of Kate's life into clearer focus. Trivialities fell away at the realization that a miracle had occurred. Her husband was safe at home, waiting for her, and her daughter was here beside her, making difficult but good choices. That was enough. Kate was content in that moment. She'd been reminded of what mattered in life, and it wasn't running from one thing to the next, finishing stained-glass projects by their deadlines or making sure her to-do list was neatly checked off. Life was so much more and so much less all at the same time. She didn't think she'd ever take the little things for granted again, like the sound of her husband's laughter or the feel of his hand in hers. All that really mattered was showing love and appreciation to those around her, who gave so freely without asking anything in return.

Rebecca touched her arm, and she looked into her daughter's vivid blue eyes, so like her father's.

"Glad to be going home?" Kate asked.

"You have no idea."

They turned onto Smoky Mountain Road and drove up to the blue ranch-style parsonage, with its autumn-colored mums looking as cheery as ever. Kate pulled the rental car into the driveway. She hadn't been inside for what seemed an eternity. For the first time, she wondered what the Sacco brothers had done to the place.

Paul was already at the front door, with Eli right behind him. Kate hurried to hug her husband, whispering an "I love you" in his ear. Then they went inside. She needn't have worried about the state of the house, whatever it had been, because Eli had cleaned it to an immaculate condition.

"Was there any . . . damage . . . from the Saccos?" she asked him, nervous about exactly how much work he had done.

"It's a good thing you didn't see it," he said, shaking his head.

She gave his hand a squeeze.

"The police took photos and did an inventory of what they broke and what was missing."

"At least from what I could remember," Paul added. "Deputy Spencer said to give him a call if we discover anything that's missing."

"Ironic," Rebecca said, looking at her ring, "that the one thing they wanted was the one thing they never got."

Rebecca and Eli excused themselves to go for a walk, and Kate watched them as they moved up Smoky Mountain Road, immersed in conversation.

"What's up with those two?" Paul asked when Kate came to sit with him on the couch.

"They've been really close this past week."

"Really?" he said with a note of hope in his voice.

Eli was the kind of man Kate had envisioned for her daughter, and she had a fleeting hope it might work out for them. But in her head, she knew it wasn't likely just yet.

"She won't stay here." Kate voiced her thoughts out

loud. "Even if she does care for Eli, she hasn't given up her dream of acting." She brushed a strand of hair from Paul's forehead. "She won't—and shouldn't—settle for less than her dreams, and I don't think a life with a man she cares about would ever be enough to make her forget about her passion for performing."

Paul nodded his agreement and pulled Kate close. He nuzzled his face next to hers. His skin felt warm and scratchy on her cheek. She laughed.

"What's so funny?" he asked.

"I'm actually enjoying the feel of your thick chin stubble."

He grinned and ran a hand along the rough surface. "Maybe I'll grow a full beard," he said.

Kate chuckled and leaned back against his chest.

"You know what I thought about most when I was out in those woods?" Paul said into Kate's ear.

"What?"

"I thought about all the years we've been together, all the ups and downs with the kids, the churches we've served in, all the little things that used to consume me. But none of it mattered to me. The thing that kept pushing me forward was the fear that I wouldn't see you again."

"It would've killed me too," Kate said. "I kept thinking that I should know where you were, like God should tell me."

"You found me, didn't you?"

Kate nodded and closed her eyes.

WHEN REBECCA came back inside, it was without Eli. Her mascara was running where tears had fallen.

"What's wrong?" Kate asked. "Where's Eli?"

"He said he wanted to walk home," Rebecca said, then she sat down between her parents, leaning her head on her father's shoulder. "I think I just broke his heart," she said.

"What happened?" Kate asked.

"I told him it would never work between us. He's been . . . a friend," she went on. "And I'm so grateful for the help and comfort and wisdom he gave me. I've never known anyone like him."

"But?" Paul said, as he stroked his daughter's blonde hair.

"But I'm not ready to leave New York City."

Kate shot a "Didn't I tell you?" look at Paul.

"We know you aren't, honey," Paul said. "God gave you your dreams. It's only right that you pursue them."

THE KITCHEN PHONE RANG. It had been ringing practically nonstop since Kate and Rebecca had gotten home, mostly with well-wishers who had heard that Paul was home and wanted to tell her how glad they were and how they'd been praying.

"Hanlons," she said.

It was Renee Lambert. Kate could hear Kisses' high-pitched whine in the background.

"I just had to call," Renee said. "Is Paul okay? He didn't have any lasting repercussions from spending all that time in the wilderness, did he?"

"No, Renee," Kate said. "Thank you so much for calling. He's just fine. Would you like to talk to him?"

Paul was shaking his head and waving his hands from
the living room.

"Oh, I guess he can't come to the phone, right now,
Renee," Kate said with a wry lift of her eyebrow.

"Well, just tell him I'm oh so glad that he's back in one
piece. He'll get a lot of sermon material out of this one, I'll
venture."

"I'll tell him," Kate said. "Thanks for calling."

She hung up and returned to the living room.

"What was that all about?" he asked.

"Renee Lambert wanted to know if you're okay," Kate
said. "Did you want to call her back?" She looked at her
husband with a mischievous twinkle in her eye.

"I might be feeling better, but I'm not *that* much better!" Paul said with a chuckle.

Then the phone rang again. This time it was Livvy.

"What's going on?" Kate asked.

"Can you come to the Town Green?"

"Why? What's going on?"

"It's a surprise."

Kate hung up and met Paul and Rebecca's expectant
looks.

"Livvy wants us to come to the Town Green right now.
Says it's a surprise."

"*Ooh!*" Rebecca said, rubbing her hands together. "I
love surprises."

When they reached the Green, it was full of people.

Some were milling around; others were sitting on blankets strategically placed around a stage that had been set up in the middle of the park. Kate, Rebecca, and Paul meandered through the crowd in search of Livvy. Finally they caught sight of her, and she came over to them.

"What's going on?" Kate asked.

"James' band is giving a concert to raise money for the Faith Freezer program!"

Kate and Rebecca exchanged questioning looks.

"He didn't tell us that the concert was a benefit," Livvy said. "I assumed he was being a typical selfish teenager . . . but just look." She gestured toward the people gathered around.

"So, what changed your mind?" Kate asked.

"The guys from the band came over shortly after we returned home. As you know, they'd originally planned the concert for Sunday, then they decided to push it back a day so they could surprise you! They begged us to let James play with them, and then the full story came out about their idea to raise money." She beamed proudly.

"This will help immensely," Kate said. "Wow."

James and the rest of the teenagers climbed onto the stage, and the crowd cheered. James' glance landed on Kate and Livvy, and he waved.

"So, you're letting him stay in the band?" Kate asked.

Livvy nodded. "I know, we're pushovers." She laughed, and Kate joined her.

Then the song began, and a hush fell over the audience. Kate glanced across the crowd. Many sent waves of greeting and thumbs-up to Paul. She felt glad to be part of a community of people who gave so freely to one another.

When the band finished playing, the crowd burst into thunderous applause. Livvy led the Hanlons to a blanket she'd laid out near the stage. "I know you need your rest," she said to Paul.

"Are you kidding?" he said. "I'm energized!"

She laughed as the four of them sat down.

"We have a special guest in our audience," James was saying from the stage. He gestured toward Rebecca, then went on. "Rebecca Hanlon is here all the way from New York City. She's a big Broadway star. Rebecca"—he looked at her—"would you do us the honor of singing for us?"

Rebecca's mouth dropped open, and her cheeks flushed. Then she looked at her mother.

"Go up there!" Kate said. "You know you want to."

Rebecca climbed the stairs and took the mic. "What would you like to hear?" she asked the band.

James shrugged and said, "We can follow you. Whatever you know works for us."

"Do you know Andrea Bocelli and Celine Dion's 'The Prayer'?" she asked.

James nodded to the other guys, and they started to play.

Rebecca smiled at the audience, at ease in front of the large crowd. Kate leaned against her husband as the song began. It was one of the most beautiful songs she'd ever heard, and to hear her daughter singing it brought tears to

Kate's eyes. This was Rebecca's gift. There was no doubt about it. God had meant for Rebecca to share it with the world.

WHEN THEY RETURNED HOME after the concert, Kate went into the kitchen to heat up leftovers for supper. She opened the freezer and pulled out a pan of lasagna.

Rebecca cleared her throat, and Kate turned to see what she wanted. Rebecca took a seat next to her father at the kitchen table, a bottle of soda and a glass of ice water in front of her.

"This past week has reminded me of some things I'd forgotten," Rebecca said.

"Like what?" Paul asked.

"Like what faith is. I saw it every day in you, Mom. The way you never gave up on Dad." She glanced at Kate and then at Paul. "You always believed that God would show us the way. I guess I've been trying to manipulate things on my own, to force my way in even if it meant doing things that weren't the best way to get there . . ."

Her sentence drifted away, and Kate sensed that Rebecca didn't want to go over the whole discussion of the play she'd auditioned for, so she waited for her to go on.

"I've decided not to go to the callback for that off-Broadway play or any play like it. I lost sight of my faith for a while, but now I get it. I still believe that I'm meant to be an actress, but God will have to open the right doors for that to happen, and I know I can trust him with my future. After all, who loves me more than he does?"

Kate was about to voice her fears as she had so many times before—that life in New York was too dangerous for a beautiful single girl—but she bit her tongue, because as much as she hated to admit it, Rebecca was right. She was in God's hands, and there was no safer, better place to be.

Chapter Thirty-One

Kate and Paul watched as Rebecca climbed the steps of the Greyhound bus in Pine Ridge that would take her back to New York City. Kate had had Eli return Marcus' convertible to the rental company earlier when Rebecca had insisted that she couldn't manage the stick shift much less that long drive alone.

Kate searched the dark windows to see Rebecca one last time. Rebecca's face pressed against the glass just like that first day on the bus to kindergarten. Kate supposed she'd always see that image of each of her children—youngsters who needed a mother's guidance in the big dangerous world—even when they grew to be her age.

Paul placed a hand on Kate's waist and gave her a squeeze as the bus pulled away. They waved until it turned out of sight, then made their way back to Paul's pickup for the return trip to Copper Mill. They would stop on the way to deliver Kate's stained-glass window to the horse farmer who had ordered it so long ago.

Kate felt bad that it was so late, and yet she knew that

in the grand scheme of things, it really didn't matter. She'd done her best and had produced a piece she was proud of. She thought of Rebecca and her statement about not settling for less than God's best in her life. Kate understood that sentiment because she saw it in her own desire to create something beautiful.

"You know, honey...," Paul said mischievously, pulling her from her musings.

She turned to look at him.

"I've been thinking," he said. "How about I plan another camping trip to the Smokies, or maybe even the Rockies, for next spring?"

"Oh no you don't, Paul Hanlon," Kate said. "Not on your life!"

About the Author

BEFORE LAUNCHING her writing career, Traci DePree worked as a fiction editor for many of the best Christian authors in the country. While still maintaining her editing career, Traci loves creating new worlds in her novels. Her hope is that, just as in Copper Mill, Tennessee, her readers will see God's creation and inspiration within the people in their own lives. Traci is the author of the best-selling Lake Emily series, including *A Can of Peas*, *Dandelions in a Jelly Jar* and *Aprons on a Clothesline*. She makes her home in a small Minnesota town with her husband and their five children, the youngest via adoption.

Mystery and the Minister's Wife

Through the Fire
by Diane Noble

A State of Grace
by Traci DePree

A Test of Faith
by Carol Cox

The Best Is Yet to Be
by Eve Fisher

Angels Undercover
by Diane Noble

Where There's a Will
by Beth Pattillo

Dog Days
by Carol Cox

Into the Wilderness
by Traci DePree